DOG AND THE MAN

A collection of
short stories by
Phil Lawder

2

ISBN: 978-9997129-3-8

Cover design by Colin Robinson

Introduction

Over the last few years, ideas for short stories have pinged into my head. When the demon work has not got in the way, I have eased or forced them onto paper, and there they have lain, occasionally shared at open mics and writing groups.

Some come out sad, even tragic, some wistful, some funny. I guess that just depends on my mood at the time. I've deliberately mixed them up in the book.

One benefit of lockdown's forced incarceration has been the elimination of alibis, reasons not to get on with reviewing, rewriting and gathering them together.

So, here they are. I hope that you find something to fit your mood.

Phil

4

CONTENTS

6

LOOKING FOR JASPER

'That day when your Great Uncle Jasper's chipolatas won a special mention at the All-Ireland Sausage and Meat Products Fair in Limerick, ah, that was a sad day for this village.'

The tired conversation that had been rolling round Billy's Bar died down immediately. It was always the way with Egan's stories. His voice had risen to signal the start of one of his tales, just slightly, no more than a gust of wind at the window. But the reaction seemed more intense than usual. Men looked at each other, eyebrows raised, and leaned in to listen. I did too. I had waited a long time to hear the story of Jasper. Perhaps this was Egan's twenty-first birthday present to me.

Egan gazed across at me, his pale eyes glinting with tears through the smoke-hung hush. 'Before you was born, college boy. Oh, yes, before you was born. Ah, he was a fine fellow, your Great Uncle Jasper. Strong as two men. I saw him carrying two pigs on his back one market day without even a bead of sweat. And he could break a hen's neck with a flick of his wrist while downing a pint in the other hand. Pure poetry. But he was brought down so he was, like Samson before him, by a woman.' And the last word carried all the venom of a man who, we all knew, had been beaten black and blue every Saturday night for twenty years by his Mary. And still he'd wept for a fortnight when she'd fallen drunk off the bridge and drowned that night last February.

'Aye, smile if you want to, college boy.' The shining eyes fixed on me. 'But it's tragedy I'm talking here, as great as any that Shakespeare fella came up with.' We sat and waited as a burst of coughing interrupted Egan's performance.

'Gets a bit dry, the old throat, with all this talking.' He looked around in silence, empty glass in hand, until I realised and moved to the bar. Billy already had another poured, which he passed over with a wink. 'I'll be putting it on the slate. There's going to be a lot more where that came from before the evening's over.'

Then, with a smack of his lips, Egan was off again. 'Aye, he went away to Limerick a butcher and came back a hero. Mind, we knew. We knew that you couldn't get better than Jasper's sausages. Every Friday payday me and my Mary, God be good to her, we'd fry up a pound of his best pork and apple. I can still smell 'em to this day, sizzling and spurting, filling our kitchen with such an aroma, you'd 'a thought that royalty was coming to tea. And I was there in the shop, that first morning he was back. We were all gathered round, the smell of sawdust and fresh blood playing catch-me-if-you-can with our nostrils, all admiring his rosette. Gold and blue it was, perched up on the counter above the liver and the bacon. And then she walked in.

"Well now, Jasper," bold as you like in front of everyone, 'I'm hoping you've got something special lined up for me now. I quite fancy one of your big fat juicy ones, eh?" And she bursts out laughing with a laugh like a saw cutting through glass. Well, that sort of language is OK for the bar, here, among men, but not in a butcher's shop. I mean, there was a lady present, well, Mrs O'Connell from the undertakers, anyway. We didn't know where to look.

'Then we hear a kind of a wheezing noise, like a car trying to start on a cold morning, and I look up to see Jasper standing there with a grin on his face like a half-drunk grizzly bear. And he's laughing. I don't remember him ever laughing before. Took his butchering serious, did Jasper.'

Egan took another long draft and stared at me. 'Aye, your great-uncle, college boy.' I half shrugged. In this village every older man was everyone else's great-uncle, a catch-all term that avoided complicated and often embarrassing explanations. Many years ago, I had asked, with the confidence of new-found logic, how it could be that one great-uncle of mine was also great uncle to a woman who was described as my great-aunt. My father had left the room and my mother had looked fixedly out of the window. "Well," she'd sighed, "the nights are very cold around these parts." At the time, my schoolboy logic did not stretch to unravelling this and, after my demands for explanation were rebuffed by silence, I'd lost interest and settled down to watch *Crackerjack*.

'Now, where was I?' Egan returned from his reverie.

'You were going to tell us who the woman was,' I ventured.

'Was I? Was I indeed? No, I don't think so, not just yet. I will tell you that she was a married woman, had come to the village some two years before and hitched up with – well, no, I won't say with who just yet, but he was fast becoming the laughing stock of the village, what with her antics. She'd reeled him in with two flicks of her eyelashes, poor sap, and now he was paying the price. Forever flaunting herself, throwing herself at people, she was. Never tried it with me, mind. She knew that my Mary would have knocked her into the next county if she'd even breathed on me.' There was a pause as Egan stared across the bar. 'Good looking girl, mind,' his voice softer now. 'I'll give her that, in an obvious sort of a way.'

'So, The Woman's there, doing all the wiggling and fluttering stuff that women do and Jasper, he's just lapping it up. Goes as scarlet as a bantam's tail feathers. Well, I bought the half-pound of streaky that I'd come in for. Gave the man a straight look as I paid the money, as if to say, *What are you thinking of, you great lummox?* But he just grinned back at me, his cheeks folded back into his double chin like curtains hanging round an old piano keyboard.

'I'll be seeing you round at Billy's later,' I called as I left. No reply came. Sure enough, that evening, Jasper's extra-large chair by the fire, just over there, remained empty.'

Another long pause followed. The glass was refilled, the pipe relit. I knew the way these things went. All my life I had listened to the stories from the old men and women of this village. They had a certain rhythm, could not be hurried. It was a skill, born of generations, that many of my lecturers in Liverpool could usefully learn. I came back here for many reasons, especially now that my ma was on her own, but the stories were one of the main ones.

But no one had ever told of Jasper before, though many still referred to the shop that had, in quick succession, been a sweet shop, a café and, with the arrival of the tourists, an antique shop, as 'Jasper's as was'. Each time I had asked about who Jasper had been, a faraway look had appeared in their eyes but no story had followed. And now here he finally was, without even a fanfare, living and breathing in Egan's words.

'Well,' Egan took up the story again. 'It was about ten o'clock when young Gerry O'Donnell came in to say that Jasper could be seen clinging for dear life to the drainpipe that ran down the side of The Woman's house. That pub emptied faster than if the Garda had been coming through the back door, as they did that time in '58. Her house was some way off, but we were there before the taste of the last swig of beer had faded. And, sure enough, there he was. As we stared up, breathless, the drainpipe, as if waiting for the audience, slowly eased away from the wall. With a shout of despair and fury, Jasper was deposited onto the garden shed, which quickly gave up the struggle to hold him and collapsed sideways with all the grace of a fat ballerina. Silence. Then, echoing out came a groan would have wakened the dead and yer man appeared, covered in compost, weeds and I won't say what else.

'Well, we should not have laughed. And we certainly should not have clapped. I suppose we felt the poor man might have been dead and we were just showing our pleasure at seeing him there. He, on the other hand, showed no such pleasure. He shook his fist at us and was gone into the night. However much we called after him, no reply came and we considered, all in all, that a pint in a warm bar was better than a confrontation on a dark night with an angry and frustrated butcher.

'Back at the bar, Gerry told all. It seems that he'd been hanging around near the butcher's shop, no doubt looking for something to pinch. He seemed to make a career out of hanging around, that Gerry O'Donnell. Well, about half past seven, Jasper emerges from his flat above the shop looking like one of his own turkeys all dressed up for Christmas. His hair, which usually had a mind of its own and seemed to be constantly making a bid for freedom, is smarmed and lathered down so that it shines like old leather. And his shirt is buttoned up, to the very top button, would you believe, for the first time in living memory, with the collar being helped in its gargantuan efforts to hold in that neck by a tie. And not just a tie but a bow tie. Now where on earth would he have got something like that from? That's the risk of going to these fancy places like Limerick, or Liverpool for that matter, college boy. You be careful you don't pick up such daft habits.

'Anyway, Jasper sets off down the road, Gerry in hot pursuit, dodging from doorway to doorway like the little ferret that he is. Then, to Gerry's astonishment, the big man turns into the churchyard. Now, Jasper attended mass each week like the rest of us but I would not have accused him of taking it seriously. Just a kind of insurance policy, you know, but an hour a week is a fair premium.

'Instead of going into the church itself, he veers off into the churchyard and Gerry sees him weaving among the gravestones, occasionally bending down. *Funny time of night to be paying your respects*, thinks Gerry but then Jasper emerges. Clutched in his fist is a bunch of flowers. Now, this is a fist that the Good Lord made to guide a cleaver through a cow's head and the thought of it reduced to carrying flowers, well, it's just not natural.

'So, Jasper sets off down the road again, the flowers flopping around in his hand like a feather duster on a windy day, Gerry in creepy pursuit. And this time, his destination is clear. Within a few minutes he's walking up the path of Yer Woman's house.

'Now, you need to know that The Woman's poor long-suffering husband was a travelling salesman. In ladies' toiletries, I think he called them. I mean, what kind of a job is that for a grown man? Anyway, he'd set off every Tuesday morning with his Morris Traveller loaded to the gunnels with whatever froufrous and folderols he'd been able to get hold of and didn't get back until Friday afternoon. You might say that was asking for trouble, college boy, with a wife like that, and I might agree with you there. But that's how it was and, this being a Wednesday, Jasper knew that the coast was clear.

'By now, Jasper's sweating freely and the hair is reasserting its independence with bits breaking free in all directions. But he strides up the path like a true knight of old only instead of the sword he is clutching the flowers, which now, with every ounce of life squeezed out of them, are hanging their heads as if for shame of the whole situation.

'He rings the bell and waits. Nothing. Nothing. Rings again and eventually, but not before Jasper's had a chance to sweat another two pints, she appears.

"Why, Jasper," she cries, "what a lovely surprise."

"But didn't you ask me round for eight o'clock?"

"Yes, and you're ten minutes early, you sweet man. And are these darling flowers for me, then? And did you choose them yourself?" And she gives him a peck on the cheek.

'A sound comes from Jasper that is not quite human speech, a sort of low rumbling groan.

"Would you be coming in then?"

'He nods a reply and follows her in. Now, this is the point where, as they used to say in the News of the World, Gerry should have made his excuses and left. But not him. In a trice he's crouched at the living room window, watching as she plies the poor sod with sweet sherry. I mean, sweet sherry for God's sake. Excuse the blasphemy but this was a man who looked naked if he didn't have a pint mug in his hand. And I knew from a rather messy episode some Christmases back, that, while he could take ten pints without blinking, two sweet sherries and he was away with the fairies.

'And so it was. I will not impose the details on your delicate young ears but suffice to say that the action relocated upstairs quite quickly. And it was while Gerry was up the drainpipe peering in the bedroom window that he sees the headlights coming down the road. Now Gerry's a bit of a mechanic when he needs to earn an honest penny for a change, and he knows the headlights and engine note of a Morris Traveller.

'Quick as a flash he's back down the drainpipe and takes his grandstand seat, or crouch, in the front garden behind the ornamental flowering cherry.

'At the sound of the car's wheels on the gravel he hears the cries upstairs change to screams and curses. Before the car door is open, she's at the front door, a negligee flying around her, looking for all the world like a giant jellyfish.

"Well, hello, darling. I wasn't expecting you back tonight. I was just about to have myself a bath and an early night. But it's such a fine night, what about a walk down the road together."

"I hardly think you're dressed for it, dear."

"So, what brings you home?" She is positioned, one arm across the front door, doing her best to look alluring and barely managing frightening.

"Sold out. Had a customer in Cork who took twenty of everything. Just won on the races and felt the need to branch out. Now, may I come into my own house, please."

'Her laugh explodes like a horse that's been kicked in the knackers. "Of course, darling, but what about a turn round the garden first."

"No, I'm tired and just want my pipe and slippers." And you don't have to be a fancy psychiatrist to see where the problems were in that marriage.

'Well, you can guess the rest. As they finally go into the house, Jasper emerges from the upstairs window, makes a grab for the drainpipe and Gerry scurries down to Billy's to tell all.

'The next morning, there's no sign of life at the shop. The day comes and goes but Jasper doesn't. In the course of the morning it becomes clear that The Woman has also disappeared, along with the Morris Traveller. Her man seems more upset at the loss of the car than of the wife.

'And that is the end of the story. Or nearly. Life in the village continues, of course, but we all still mourn to this day the loss of that fine butcher and his All-Ireland beating sausages. Stories and rumours came and went. They'd gone to sea on the Queen Mary, opened a pub in Kilkenny, even that they'd gone to England. Then the most extraordinary thing happens. It turns out that this meek and mild husband of hers had another woman on the go just twenty miles down the road, so she moves in. Well, we're a bit shocked at first, didn't think he had it in him. But, do you know, she's such a fine sweet lady we take to her soon enough, out of relief at seeing the back of the other one as much as anything.

'Then, two years later, the husband comes back one day from his travels with an extra load in his new shiny car. A little bundle of a baby it is. Seems the poor fella's been firing blanks all this time and has had to go for a take-away. Now, college boy,' the eyes fixed on me again, 'would you be telling me who the baby was then?'

I was already there. The travelling salesman, the flowering cherry tree in the front garden, even the drainpipe that still wobbled in high winds after all these years.

'It was me.' I heard a collective sigh run round the bar as everyone stopped holding their breath.

'That's right, Sean.' He used my name for the first time that evening. 'Your ma asked me to tell you about all this, you know. Felt it would be better coming from a man. And I am your great-uncle, after all. How do you feel about what you've heard?'

I thought about the question. 'OK. I feel OK. I mean, I always knew that there was something, what with everyone saying that I didn't look a bit like either of them, being twice their size and all. But I think there's more that you want to tell me, isn't there?'

Egan smiled, the three remaining teeth in his head glinted at me. 'You're bright, sure enough, college boy. Just before your da passed on last year he told me the rest of it. It seems that Jasper and The Woman did settle in Kilkenny and ran the pub there. Famous, it was, for the meals. But Jasper was not a well man. I think he was grieving for his shop and the old life here. Still, he was well enough to sire a babe. Well, the babe appears and herself is more interested in getting her beauty sleep than caring for it. So, he's up every night as well as running the pub single-handed. One morning, about three months after the baby appears, The Woman wakes up, the babe's screaming and Jasper's nowhere to be seen. She finds him downstairs, laid out in the kitchen, bottle of baby milk still in his hand.

'Well, it's a fine funeral, though it took ten men to carry the coffin. She recovers soon enough – that type does – and by the end of the wake she's already fluttering at some rich old bookie. He's keen but not with the babe, so she makes a call to your da.'

I looked down at my hands, great fat digits that had embarrassed me as long as I could remember. Could they, I wondered, lift two pigs, strangle hens? For the first time, they looked right; strong, trustworthy hands. I stood up and walked across to the big chair by the fire, Jasper's chair, and sat down. It seemed to wrap itself around me. I looked across to Egan.

'Your round, I think, old fella.'

CLOSE YOUR EYES AND I'LL KISS YOU

She was everything that the Beach Boys had promised. Blonde, tanned, freckles scattered over a face for which the word 'cute' had been invented. She even had flowers in her hair; one hibiscus bloom was tucked casually behind each ear. The perfect 60s babe. She sat at the back of the Greyhound bus, chewing gum and staring out of the side window. On the wall of the bus stop diner opposite hung a poster covered in swirls and wild colour, advertising The Byrds and The Mamas & the Papas at the Fillmore West, July 24th.

As I stepped onto the bus, the air conditioning bit into my skin, the July heat's sweat congealing instantly. There were a couple of empty seats on the way through to the back, but I was focused. I swung my backpack onto the overhead rack and dropped down into the seat beside her.

I gave her my opening shot. 'Is it always this hot in Pasadena?'

She turned towards me, clear pale blue eyes assessing me.

'You must be British.'

'Is it that obvious,' I deflated.

'No one but a Brit would start a chat-up with talking about the weather.' She smiled, a living advertisement for orthodontics.

I tried innocence. 'Was I chatting you up?'

'How many seats did you pass to sit here?'

'But how do you know. You were looking out of the window.'

She raised an eyebrow. As well as all their other attributes, American girls clearly had the peripheral vision of a bluebottle. Her expression changed to something depressingly close to pity.

'Hi, anyway, I'm Beth.' She held out a hand that I seized like a drowning man making a grab for the last lifebelt.

'Charles,' I muttered. 'Er, that's Charlie, really, well, here it is …'

'That's OK, Charles. Your secret is safe with me. Don't tell me, you're an English kid from a rich home, pretending you're the son of a duke or something, so you can impress the dumb colonials and get laid a few times before you have to go back home to tea and crumpets. Am I right?'

'Pretty close,' I grinned. 'You just missed out the bit about being related to the Beatles.'

I was rewarded with another thousand-watt smile. 'I like you, Charlie, but don't get your hopes up. I'm in enough trouble already without you making things more complicated.'

While we had been talking, the bus had pulled out and was now rolling down the main street towards the highway.

'So, tell me, Charlie, what have you been doing here in California. Actually, no, don't tell me. I'm really not interested.'

'I got to the concert last night. The one you were looking at the poster of, back at the stop.'

'Yea,' she replied, showing little interest. 'I was there too.'

'Wasn't it amazing?' I enthused, completely forgetting to be cool.

'I guess.' This was clearly another conversation not to pursue. Nevertheless, I blundered on.

'Hey, we could have met there.'

She was looking out of the window. 'I don't think so. I was backstage.'

Game, set and match, Charlie, old son. You are really out of your depth here. Silence fell. I looked out of the window. We were on the highway now, raised up, swinging past the endless retail stores and fast food stops that cluster like parasites around the edge of every American town. On top of Honest Joe's Bed-Land, a ten-foot high fibreglass cowboy waved jerkily, his gesture somehow obscene. On Sambo's Pancake House, several lights had failed and the sign now shouted out the wonders of Sab's Pacak Hou.

With the stubborn determination of a lemming, I tried again. 'So, what kind of trouble are you in?'

'Huh?' She had nearly been asleep.

'You, er, mentioned that you were in trouble. I just wondered, what kind of trouble.'

'Charlie, when a girl says she's in trouble, that can only mean one thing. Surely, even in England, they still have sex sometimes, even if it's to keep the cold out.'

'Oh, I see.'

'Ah, come on, man, don't look so down. It's a bummer but it's not your problem. Sure, you had it all figured out, how your English charm and good looks would sweep me off my tush and how you and I would go travelling the States together, living by our wits, sharing adventures and motel rooms. Well, my English friend Charlie, it's not going to happen.'

She was right, of course. I remembered my grandmother saying, frequently, 'Charles, if you can't think of anything intelligent to say, say nothing and preserve the illusion.' Too late already, but I silently took out the book that I kept for such emergencies, Kerouac's *On the Road*. She didn't even laugh, just looked, shook her head, closed her eyes and went to sleep.

One silent hour later, I had managed three pages of Kerouac. Afternoon was easing into a thick, muggy evening. The highway was full of people going home to their neat little houses. I envied them. The bus pulled off the road. Beth stirred.

'Come on, Charlie, you can buy me a coffee.' She stood up and stretched, reminding me why I had sat there in the first place. I followed her into the roadside diner and to a booth by the window.

An elderly woman approached, her grudging limp and down-turned mouth belying the cheerfulness of the frilly apron, the bobby socks and the hat that read 'Hi, I'm Freda'.

'Yea?'

'Oh, good evening,' I started. 'We'd like, please, let's see …'

'Two coffees, two slices of pumpkin pie,' Beth cut in. 'God, you Brits! How many thousands of you die of hunger before you've placed your order?'

I shrugged. 'Only a couple of hundred a year. You find them slumped in railway booking halls and little country tea-rooms, muttering "I wonder if you'd be so kind, if it's not too much bother" with their last breath.' Over the last few weeks, I had become very adept at mocking my own race and, by association, myself.

The pie arrived, placed in front of us without a word. 'Gee, thanks, honey,' beamed Beth. A grunt was all she got in reply.

'OK, Charlie. That old bitch has got it coming to her. Here's what we do. When you go up to pay, give her a twenty. You got a twenty?' I nodded. 'Leave the rest to me.'

'What do you mean?'

'Watch and learn, kid. Watch and learn.'

Plates cleaned and coffee drained, I walked over to the till. Beth followed close behind me. The till was on a stand at the end of the counter. Beside it were boxes of candies and a tall pyramid stand full of lollipops.

'Two dollars, ten.' I pulled out my wallet and offered over the twenty-dollar bill.

'Ain't you got nothing smaller?'

I shook my head. The old waitress sighed, a sigh that expressed her full opinion of twenty-dollar bills, English punks and the lousy hand that life had dealt her. She jabbed the buttons on the till and the drawer flew open.

Beth leaned forward. 'Oh, hey, I'll have one of these lollipops too. That green one right up there.' She reached up and, as she did so, slipped and the whole structure fell over, scattering lollipops in all directions. Beth scrambled round the end of the counter, full of apologies, as I bent to pick up the ones that had fallen on my side.

'Leave it, leave it!' shouted the waitress. 'Just get the hell out of here before you break anything else.' She thrust the change into my hand and Beth and I made for the door.

Outside, I turned to her. 'What was that all about?'

'I'll show you on the bus,' she grinned.

Once we were back in our seats, she suddenly grabbed my hand and pushed it down the front of her dress. 'Grab some of that,' she whispered. It was not what I expected. My hand emerged, a little reluctantly, grasping a bunch of notes.

'Count it,' she commanded, as the bus door hissed shut and the engine started, sending a shudder up through the seats.

In my hand were forty-five dollars in crumpled notes. She rummaged around and found another twenty.

'That's twenty-five for you and forty for me. Sound like a fair split?' She lifted her share out of my hand and slipped it into the little red purse that she carried at her waist. I looked at the remainder, then looked back at her. I did not speak for a long time.

'Who are you?' I finally managed.

'Why, Charlie, I'm just an all-American gal. You know, pioneer spirit, resourceful, plucky, as you would say. Now, close your mouth and put the money away.'

Looking nervously around, I stuffed the bills into the back pocket of my jeans. Over the next few hours, we talked endlessly, our shared crime creating a bond between us as strong as the Hole in the Wall Gang. We talked about rock music, California, Vietnam, student unrest, about everything except her. And the more we talked, the less I knew about Beth. And I was never going to know. Just before midnight, we pulled into a small town on the border of California and Nevada.

'This is me,' said Beth abruptly, jumping to her feet. 'Bye, Charlie Englishman.' She pulled down her bag. 'Oh, now, don't you go looking so down. Come here.' And she held out her arms. I stood up awkwardly from the seat and we hugged for a few seconds. She closed her eyes when she kissed me, though whether from passion or lack of interest was impossible to tell. Then she picked up her bag and set off down the aisle. With a little wave, she was down the steps and gone. I watched as she walked over to a middle-aged couple, both wearing matching plaid shirts and jeans. Then the bus pulled out and it was over.

I pushed my hand into my back pocket. The twenty-five dollars were gone. I laughed aloud. Well, fair's fair. In my other pocket were the forty dollars that I had lifted from her purse during our conversation. After all, even the sons of 'dooks' have to eat.

PLANNING FOR RETIREMENT

'If you think you can pack me off to fester and rot in Budleigh bloody Salterton, Sunny Jim, you've got another think coming.'

Across my desk, his watery blue eyes glare up from under straggling grey eyebrows. The mouth is a tight, lipless line. I've seen the look many times before. The classic interrogation stare that the Firm has been teaching us since it was founded. But, beneath it, imperceptible to all but a few of us, something else. Deep lines dive and swirl around his face. There are wisps of stubble below his chin and under the cheekbones. The slight shake of the hand as he lights his third cigarette, the eyes sliding away from contact at the last moment. Yes, I was right. It is time.

I allow a smile. 'I can sympathise with you about Budleigh Salterton. I had a great-aunt who lived there. Dire.' I watch as he tries to disguise the surprise. I'm used to that. No, I haven't just got off the boat. 'So, go where you want. Except back to your region, of course. You know the rules. What about the South of France? Great way of life, I'm told.'

He waves his arm dismissively. 'Full of poofs and gigolos.' He drags deeply on his cigarette, then leans in towards me, spraying the acrid smoke at me like a poisoned gas attack. This must be the only place left in London where a man can smoke in the office, in this case my office. But we always did make our own rules. I lean back.

'Look,' his voice rises, 'you're still not getting the point. I've worked the Arab sector for thirty-three years. I've seen us through two Arab-Israeli wars, God knows how many changes of so-called government in God knows how many so-called countries. I've built and rebuilt networks. If ever you lot needed that experience it's now, now that the towel-heads have brought the fight to you.'

I let the silence hang heavy. Towel-heads. Yes, my friend, and that's why your days are over. That's why no one of my generation will have anything to do with you. They can smell it on your breath.

He looks up sharply at me. 'No slight intended, old chap.' He attempts a smile. 'I mean, you're one of us, after all. Winchester and Oxford, wasn't it? Sorry, one drops into the vernacular after a while. But seriously, though, you need my knowledge.'

'Well, we will certainly call on you when we need to.' We both know it is a lie and I know he will not dare to challenge it. I am getting bored with the conversation. There's limited pleasure to be had from watching someone swinging in the wind, deprived of his only reason for existing. What am I offering him, after all? A few years of close companionship with the whisky bottle, cornering bored, disbelieving strangers in musty bars? Well, sympathy is not useful in my profession.

'So, who are you planning to slip into my place?'

'You know I can't tell you that.'

'As long as it's not that bloody little shit Wasik.'

'As I said, I can't tell you that.'

He stares at me, the cigarette half raised to his lips. Ash drops on the lapel of his crumpled suit; he doesn't notice.

'It is, isn't it? It's bloody Wasik. My God, you lot really do stick together, don't you? Scratching each other's swarthy backs.'

I watch the colour rise in his face.

'Look, Ahmed, or whatever your name is, you may be making the decisions here but you're nothing but a bloody desk jockey. What the hell do you know about being out there? The most dangerous thing you've ever done is to get a fish paste sandwich from the canteen downstairs. What the hell do you know about any of it?'

I could tell him what I know. I could tear off this clean white shirt and show him the scars. I could tell him about screams in the dark, the smell of burning flesh, the hopeless blackness of a stinking cell. But no. That is not how we do things in the Firm.

I put down my pen. 'You will be escorted back next week to collect your things and will be put on pension effective from the first of next month. I take it you are familiar with the secrecy contract.'

'All eighty-five pages, sonny.'

I pull a copy from my drawer and push it over to him.

'Please return this to the department with your signature by tomorrow night.'

He glares back at me, arms folded, not touching the document. I wait. Ten seconds, I guess. He picks it up after eight and leaves without another word.

I walk over to the window, pushing it open to rid my office of the smell of cigarette smoke. Returning to my desk, I finish filling in the form on my screen. He would need to be watched. Given the budget problems in the department at the moment, it would be better if he didn't tie up one of our people. Anyway, which bright young graduate is going to want to spend his time trailing this knackered old warhorse from bar to bar?

I tick the box that will ensure that he does not reach pension day and press send.

26

TOO MUCH REALITY

I suppose that my big mistake was telling other people about it. But that's how it is in my profession. We share our findings. Seminars, books, papers, all that twaddle. We all claim, modestly, that it's for the common good of mankind. Ironic, really, considering the outcome. No, I should just have kept quiet and indulged my little habit. Taken my findings with me to the grave.

But I'm jumping ahead, and I can see that you're already getting fidgety. Your left foot is starting to tap, and you have shifted position in your seat three times in the last two minutes. That's what I do, you see, I observe. Can't kick the habit. Thirty years of watching people, recording their every move and I know what everyone is thinking. Intolerable burden, you know. Maybe that's why I shared it with others, actually. Nothing to do with the common good, after all.

Oh, I'm sorry, off on a tangent again. Focus, Wolverton, focus. And that's another thing. With a name like mine, I mean, the media were always going to love it, weren't they? 'And here, with another of his potty theories that are going to destroy mankind, is Wolverton Poultney.' You could just hear the smirk in their voices, especially on radio.

Sorry, I know, but I have a very discursive mind. Also known as wandering, rambling or infuriatingly vague. I remember a report card at school; 'Poultney may do well if he ever allows his mind to settle on a topic for more time than it takes to boil an egg.' Rather clever, in a bitchy, condescending sort of schoolmasterly way. He was right, though. Mind you, now, of course, I wish I hadn't. Settled on a subject, I mean. We wouldn't all be in this awful mess, would we?

My early work was all fairly harmless, really. Just building on the studies that Mass Observation had carried out in the war. You know, how families, so-called ordinary people, live their lives, people's reaction to world events, all that stuff. Then I realised that there was serious money to be made in the commercial sector, working for the big marketing companies, so I sold my soul to the devil and went for it. You know the sort of thing, getting people to give up their innermost thoughts about their relationship with their washing powder or what sexual fantasies are fulfilled by the length of the bonnet on their car.

It was great fun to start with, genuinely, even though I was never able to take it totally seriously. I'd be sitting there, debriefing these terribly earnest little businessmen about why their latest idea was a complete stinker and they would be writing everything down and nodding like toy dogs. I would think, *Come on, lads, don't take the word of some pompous academic* – and I was rather pompous, you know – *some academic who's spoken to a couple of dozen randomly selected women and so now claims to be a world expert. If you believe in your idea, just do it.* But they didn't. Probably looking for reasons not to do anything, stay safe.

Frankly, if the clients didn't bother to turn up to the research groups, I made most of it up anyway. Gave me a rather nice feeling of power. I'd even leave them with the tape recordings of the group discussions, which would totally contradict my findings. But I knew they would never listen to them. Then I'd call up a few days later: 'What did you think of the tapes?' 'Oh, yes, very interesting, Dr Poultney. They really bear out the points you made in your presentation.' Well, you can't feel sorry for them, can you?

But, you know, after a while these things all get a bit samey. When you're sitting there getting a bunch of women to decide whether some household cleaner represents their mother or their big sister or whether they'd let their daughter go on a date with a certain brand of yoghurt, the mind does tend to wander. Self-defence, I suppose, hanging onto some semblance of sanity. So, I started to work out who was lying and who was telling the truth. Some of it was obvious. 'Oh, no, I never use a spray polish, it's bad for the ozone layer, you know,' and you find they've got twenty of the things under the sink. Or 'I take real pride in sending my husband off with a clean white shirt each morning' and then you see the poor scruffy bugger picking her up at the end.

That was the easy stuff, quite honestly. But then I started to look at the body language. Such a treasure trove. We all know that pulse rate increases when you lie; that's how lie detectors work, why you blush and so on. But there's so much more to it. Blink rate is a good one. I've seen people blink at a rate of sixty a minute when they're telling a whopper, but some people knew about that one too, so I had to look for more subtle signals. Shoulders are a big give-away. When people lie, one shoulder edges up higher than the other. Do you know, it's always the left shoulder for right-handed people? Fascinating. No idea why, but truly fascinating.

But why am I telling you all this? You know already. Everyone knows. I suppose it's just my missionary zeal. Or that need to share the burden. So, you know all about the other signals – hunching the back, uncrossing the legs, tugging the earlobe, scratching the nose, the yawn, the stretch, all that stuff. After a couple of years of these mind games, I'd got it down to a T. By then, of course, I was getting quite well known anyway as a talking head. Anything to do with the iniquities of advertising or trends in modern housewifery and old Wolverton Poultney would be trundled out to pontificate. And my publishers were nagging for another book. Only fair, since they had already given me the advance and I had already spent it. So, I thought, let's have a bit of fun with this little game of mine.

Well, poor old Pandora had nothing on me. I remember, I sent in the manuscript and a couple of days later had a call from the editor's assistant.

'Oh, Dr Poultney, Mr Johnson has asked me to call you to thank you for the manuscript. He really enjoyed it.' Now, this was strange, because David Johnson is an old friend and he always calls me himself.

'Oh, right. Um, how is David,' I replied. 'Not unwell, I hope.'

There was a nervous giggle at the other end.

'Actually, he told me to say that he was out, but I've looked at your manuscript and I know you'd be able to tell I was lying. The truth is, Dr Poultney, he really can't pick up the phone to you. He's afraid that you'll know his inner secrets, whatever they are. And he said something about your wife and a weekend at a book fair in Frankfurt, but I didn't really catch that.'

That's when I should have recalled the manuscript and burnt it. But, of course, you don't, do you? Things trundled on relentlessly and, before I knew it, we were at the launch party, with David Johnson, I noticed, hovering at the furthest corner of the room. Well, the press soon heard about it and, very quickly, it had changed from a semi-academic treatise entitled *The Physiognomy of Untruth* to the blockbuster serialised in the Daily Mail called *Trust No One*. Not my idea.

At first, though, I quite enjoyed the celebrity. Even got on Graham Norton. Had great fun with all his tics; maybe you saw me. But then, of course, it all started to unravel. Everyone became an expert at telling if someone was lying. Except that they weren't experts, of course, because you need years of practice. People were having stand-up fights in the streets, divorce rates rocketed, the advertising industry vanished overnight, the health service was in complete turmoil and businesses were crashing by the day. So far, eleven million are out of work, many of them on the streets. As for politics, well, when was the last time you saw the Prime Minister on television? So, not all bad, I suppose.

But, seriously, it appears that I have single-handedly destroyed the whole fabric of our society. I realise now that we need to lie to each other to survive. What was it T.S. Eliot said, something about humankind not being able to bear too much reality? Well, I've certainly proved that. At the last count, I have one thousand, three hundred and eighty-six lawsuits pending against me for destroying lives and livelihoods. And that's not counting the thousands and thousands of poisonous letters, phone calls and texts that I've received. Thank God I never went onto social media. None of my friends even talk to me and my wife left me ages ago. Even the dog seems to be avoiding me.

So that's why I end up accosting people like you in bus shelters. Well, you've been very patient, and I have made you miss three buses, so it's only fair that I let you go now. Goodnight and please, please don't tell me that it was nice to meet me.

SATURDAY IN THE CAFÉ IN THE PARK

He sees her bent forward, crying. A stranger but, at the same time, the hard grip of familiarity.

A warm Saturday, the café full of the hiss of the espresso machine, screeching kids, swirling conversations. Sitting with a friend, chewing on suburban scandals. Then, just a glimpse, like you sometimes get from a train, half hidden by the tables between them. Her, staring at the table, tears falling down a face that's as crumpled as the tissues in her hand. Husband, has to be a husband, not a lover, he has that look of the dutiful, sad-eyed hound waiting unquestioning at his lady's door. He rubs her back as if she has indigestion, glancing around, embarrassed and challenging. And the child, playing self-consciously, holding a loud conversation with her teacup, sure it is somehow her fault.

From his safe distance, the man watches. Wants to take her hand through the fearful carapace that holds her trapped and tell her, 'This too will pass'. To do what he was unable to all those years ago. Decisiveness has never come easy. More a man to weigh up options than point the way. Finally though, he eases back his chair. Half stands.

He realises that his friend has just asked about a television show he hasn't seen and is waiting for a response. He hesitates, and the moment has gone. He sits, leans back in, feels that same sense of helplessness deep in his gut.

'Only connect.' Who was that? Goethe? Voltaire? Should remember, all those years with his head buried in books, the world coming to him through the written word. Or going away from him. Held at bay. He picks up his cappuccino and delivers the expected funny stories. When he looks across again, they are gone.

Redemption will have to wait.

34

THE FAREWELL PARTY

'For God's sake, Charles, we're only going to be a quarter of an hour late.'

'Only? You know the old man. Punctuality is next to godliness for him.'

'Yes, well, your father had the help of half a battalion when he had to shift you lot around. I have an au pair with barely half a brain.'

The car was hot, the glare from the sun oppressive and my sunglasses were sitting neatly on my desk back home. In the back, the boys took it in turns to ask 'Are we there yet?' and to moan about the journey. That freaky Peppa Pig character had ceased to work her dubious magic before we were even out of London and had left me with a strong desire to strangle something small and furry.

At last, we reached the small Cotswold village, a world so different from the noise and dirt of our East London street. I swung the car gratefully onto the gravel drive that curved round in front of my father's house. We were exactly fourteen minutes late.

'I'll go in and let him know we are here. You bring in the kids,' I muttered to Jane without looking at her. I stepped out of the car and looked up at the white Edwardian frontage, shielding my eyes from the glare of the midday sun. The steep gables soared upwards with the confidence of an empire and the large windows spoke defiantly of a time before heat conservation had even been thought of, when there were always logs for a roaring fire. Why don't they let me design places like this nowadays instead of making me slave away, watching every ounce of creativity being annihilated by forty-seven different EU regulations?

For most people, the house of their childhood shrinks as they grow up. Not so for me. This house, like my father, seemed to grow larger and more contemptuous of my efforts.

I crunched across the gravel to the double front door with its original stained glass. Well, nearly original. A mis-kicked football had shattered glass and landed me in trouble many years ago. I had often been reminded of how long it had taken to find a craftsman who could repair it.

My father appeared at the door, clad as always in his cord trousers and Barbour jacket.

'Ah, Charles. Excellent, and only a little late. Quite good for you, really. How was the journey? Bloody, I expect, in this heat. Come through to the back, I'm just finishing something.' And with that he was gone. I followed his tall, upright frame as he marched through the house to the conservatory.

I could hear them straight away. A low rumble of sounds that grew rapidly as I crossed the drawing room that smelled, as always, of leather books and furniture polish. As I stepped down into the conservatory, I could make out the shouts of children, women calling to each other. I looked out into the garden. My father was weaving his way between the shrubs and rose bushes, oblivious to the children who ran around him and the men and women who stood chatting in groups.

I had seen them once before. It had been a day very like this, at this time of year. I was seven. We had just returned from a tour of duty in Aden and my mother and I had both picked up some exotic and rather aggressive bug. Mother was in hospital but my attack was much milder, so I was left in my father's care. 'Plenty of fresh English air, that's what the boy needs' had been my father's prognosis and I had been put outside every afternoon to lie in the soft English sun. I had woken to find myself in the middle of a garden party. Women with their best hats, men with tightly buttoned collars, in spite of the warmth. The clothes. I noticed it with the children first. All the children that I had seen around the village, boys and girls, spent the summer in aertex shirts and shorts. But these boys wore knickerbockers and smart white shirts, while the girls were in long smocked dresses with ribbons in their hair.

I jumped off the camp bed and ran down to talk to them. A boy of about ten stopped and stared at me.

'Who are you?'

'My name is Charles Callendar,' I replied. 'I live here.'

'No, you don't. Old Miss Johnson lives here. She's the one who invited us to this farewell party.'

'Farewell party? What's that?'

'Where you from?' The boy's eyes narrowed. 'I ain't seen you round here. You a spy, then?'

Before I could reply, I heard my nurse calling to me as she ran down the lawn. 'Charles, Charles, what are you doing? Who are you talking to?'

I turned to her. 'To this boy, of course.'

'What boy?'

I turned back. 'Well, him …' There was no one there. The garden was deserted.

The doctor put it down to a 'touch of the sun'. I tried to explain to my father what I had seen but he was distracted with worry about my mother. His only response was 'Yes, well, these foreign bugs are damn tricky fellows. Knew someone once who thought he was a rhinoceros.'

The following day my mother died. I don't think I ever had another real conversation with my father after that day. No more was said about my invisible friends. However much I longed to see them again, they never returned. Until today.

'Charles, come and look at my roses.' My father's voice jerked me back to the present and I walked down the lawn to join him. The figures swirled around me, but I did not dare to speak to them for fear that they would disappear again.

'Come on Charles, snap out of it. You dreaming of those tower blocks you build? No room for that here. Look, what do you think of those? Best show I've had for years. Managed to keep the damned aphids off this year.'

'They're great, Dad. And how are you.'

'Oh, fine, fine.' The awkward silence that fell between us was broken by the shouts of my two boys as they charged across the lawn to greet their grandfather.

'Grandpa, Grandpa, can we build a den? Are we having some of Mrs Blaney's chocolate cake for tea? Is the train set still up in the attic?'

'Hold your horses, my boys. Now, come with me into the house and I'll see if I've got a nice cool drink for you.'

I watched them walk back to the house, the boys' patterned shirts and jeans contrasting so strongly with the more formal outfits of the children only I could see. I stood alone among the roses.

'Hello, Charlie.' The voice was softened by the gentle Oxfordshire accent. 'How you been keeping?' I turned to see a girl of about eight with wide blue eyes set in a face browned by the sun.

'Do I know you,' I dared to whisper.

She laughed. 'No, I suppose you don't. But we know you. We've been expecting you.'

'What's happening?'

'You'll find out. Go to the pub. Talk to Billy. Tell him Sadie sent you.'

I walked back into the house. Jane was ushering the boys into the kitchen while keeping up a conversation with my father about aphids and ladybirds.

'I, um, I need some fresh air,' I announced. 'I'll be back in a little while.'

'Well, there's plenty of air here, Charles,' my father grunted. Jane shot me an irritated look. I backed out of the front door and scurried down the drive.

The pub was only a five-minute walk away. My request for a half of cider was greeted by the landlord with a raised eyebrow. I muttered about having to drive and paid. It took my eyes a minute to adjust to the smoke-hung gloom. There were a few people playing darts and two or three of the tables were occupied. I called the landlord over. With a sigh, he came towards me. I felt foolish, like a teenage boy asking for his first pint.

'Could you tell me which one is Billy, please?'

'What you want to talk to that daft old fool for?'

'I, er, there's something someone wants me to ask him.' The landlord looked at me. I could feel myself blushing.

'Over there, by the fireplace. The one who's talking to himself.'

I went across. In the corner was the bent figure of a very old man, one gnarled hand grasping a glass while the other rested on a stick. Despite the heat, he was wearing a tweed suit, which seemed to grow out of his body.

'Billy?'

He didn't look up. 'Who wants to know?'

'I'm Charles, Charles Callendar.'

'So?'

'Um, Sadie sent me.'

I saw his shoulders hunch and heard an intake of breath. Then he slowly looked up. The scowl was gone. His eyes shone and a smile started to spread across the lined face.

'You seen my Sadie? Where? In Miss Johnson's garden?'

'Well, yes, except it's not Miss Johnson's. It's my father's. It has been for about thirty years.'

'It was Miss Johnson's then, and it always will be.'

'Then? When?'

'Want to know a lot, don't you, Charles Callendar. Well, a man needs a drink if he's going to do a lot of talking.'

I was back from the bar quickly and I took a seat next to Billy.

'So, tell me. What's it all about.'

Billy looked at me for a long time, as if deciding whether to tell me.

'What do you know, then?' he asked.

I hesitated, knowing that what I was about to say would sound deranged. I took a deep breath.

'I know that I can see a lot of people in the garden. And I've seen them once before, when I was young.'

'Can they see you?'

'Yes, Sadie spoke to me. And there was a boy that spoke to me before, a lad of about ten, red hair, freckles.'

'I expect that would be Harry Smith.'

'Oh, and he said something about a farewell party.'

'So you know it all, don't you?'

'I do?'

'Bloody hell, lad. I thought you city boys was supposed to be bright.'

'But, what? What am I missing?'

'How were they dressed?'

'Old fashioned. 1910, 1920, about then.'

'And what was going on then?'

I thought for a moment, racking my brains for forgotten history lessons.

'Of course, the First World War.'

'Great War, we called it. The war to end all wars.'

A wave of realisation washed over me. 'So the Farewell Party was for the men who were going away.'

'Now you're thinking proper. You've read about how each town raised a regiment? Well, we did our duty here too. Every able-bodied man went off to join the Royal Oxfordshire. June 25th 1915 they went. Miss Johnson arranged the party on the 24th.'

'24th? That's today. And it must have been about then that I saw them in the garden before.'

'Exactly then.'

'What happened? I mean, what happened to the men?'

'Sent off to Turkey, they were. The ones that didn't die of the shits was all blown to pieces. All done for in the space of forty minutes because some bloody fool with a posh voice couldn't read a map properly.'

I felt a coldness creep down my spine. 'So, I've been seeing dead people.'

'Well, not all dead. You remember a little blond lad, about six year old with a blue top.'

In my mind, I could see the boy he meant running across the lawn. 'Was that you?'

Billy grinned a toothless grin. 'Changed a bit, haven't I?'

'And Sadie?'

'Lost her about a year since, God rest her. She was a good wife.' He gazed into the empty fireplace for a moment.

'So why have I seen it again today?'

'Same reason I saw it this time last year, I suppose. Now, Charles Callendar, your family will be wondering where you are. You'd better hurry on back.'

I arrived back to stony glares from Jane. My father, on the other hand, was in a chatty mood for once and I got him talking about earlier times, about my mother and the postings that he had travelled to. Eventually, it was time to go. The boys gave their grandfather big hugs, Jane pecked him on the cheek and ushered them out to the car.

My father and I eyed each other, the old wariness starting to creep back.

'You know, Dad,' I ventured, 'I've really enjoyed today. It's been,' I hesitated, 'remarkable. Yes, remarkable.'

He looked at me with surprise. 'Yes, it has, hasn't it? I've really enjoyed it too. More than I realised. Now, get on with you, or you'll get caught in the traffic.'

He walked me to the door. 'And Charles, you know, I do quite like those buildings that you design. Don't really understand them, I mean, I'm just an old war-horse, really. But, well done. Well done.' A tightness in my throat prevented me from replying. I wanted to hug him, but you can't shake off a lifetime of conditioning. I shook his hand, holding it as long as I could, and walked to the car.

As we drove out of sight, waving finished, Jane turned on me.

'Bloody hell, Charles, could you be any weirder? Wandering around like you've seen a ghost, then disappearing to the pub, for heaven's sake. There's a limit to how long I can talk about aphids, you know. And all that digging up the past. What was all that about?'

'I'll tell you tomorrow,' I replied.

The phone call that I'd been expecting came at ten-thirty the following morning. 'Oh, Mr Callendar, it's Mrs Blaney speaking.

It's the Colonel, your father. Oh, Mr Callendar, I'm so sorry. I came in just now and there he was on the floor. Heart attack, I suppose. I'm sure it was very quick.'

'That's all right, Mrs Blaney. Thank you for letting me know and I'm just so sorry you've had this horrible shock. I'll come straight away.'

Billy's words came piling back into my head. 'Same reason I saw it this time last year, I suppose', just before his Sadie had died. Everything fell into place. I felt calmer than I had for many years. I walked upstairs to where the boys were playing in their room and gave them the news.

Jack, our youngest, looked up at me. 'Daddy, has Grandpa dying got anything to do with all those people I saw on his lawn yesterday?'

CINDERELLA SHALL GO TO THE BALL

'The trouble is,' George grimaced and stared at the ceiling in silence for a moment, 'Ros is, I mean, let's face it, she is, well, really ugly. A bit of a Ros-nosaurus.'

An awkward silence fell. We both agreed, of course we did, but there's a difference between thinking something unpleasant and saying it. That said, I think it was Jilly who started giggling first, but it might have been me. George is wicked, but you can't help going along with him. And the panto is the highlight of our season, after all, and one does have to maintain a certain standard.

Ros was the mainstay of our am-dram group, ever willing, out in all weathers delivering leaflets, putting up posters, collecting props. But playing Cinderella? Ros? Well, no. Having Cinders towering over George as Prince Charming was ridiculous enough, but her weight was the real issue. It was, as George put it, a day's march to get around her. I don't know what had possessed her to put her name forward.

We knew she would be disappointed but, actually, she took it surprisingly well. I was delegated to tell her. I tried to get Jilly to do it, but it was 'No, you're the producer; that's what you wanted. I'm just costumes and scenery. You tell her.' That's wives for you, no mercy.

I phoned, rather than go head to head.

'Oh, well,' she said. 'I suppose I'm not surprised. I expect George is going to be Prince Charming and I would look odd acting against a dwarf.'

I decided that this was not the time to discuss whether George's five foot four constituted dwarfness or dwarfdom, whatever the noun is, and was happy to quickly finish the conversation.

She turned down the role of First Footman, and I have to say I was relieved. Having Ros lurking in the background in a dark mood when you're rehearsing can be a little unsettling. Always afraid she might lose her temper and sit on you.

We were going to cast young Kirsty as Cinders; she's got a good loud voice and can hold a tune fairly well. But then her mother decided that the little darling needed to concentrate on her schoolwork. Something about poor mock exams; bloody inconsiderate if you ask me.

I bumped into Ros about this time in Sainsbury's.

'How's casting going,' she asked, after the compulsory pleasantries.

'Oh, you know, getting there.'

'Hmm. Well, if ever, you know …'

'Yes, yes, of course. Thank you, Ros.'

We were not going to get that desperate. I let her get on with her shopping. Couldn't help noticing that her basket was full of meals for one, though sadly few of the slimming options. Strange, I had thought she lived with her mother, but Jilly told me that the old lady had died a couple of years ago. Ros might have mentioned it at the time, but I don't remember that sort of thing.

George found us our Cinders in the end. Pretty little thing. George seems to come across these *ingénues* quite regularly, all of them about half his age, though this one was not quite as young as she looked at first sight. He's rather vague about how and where he finds them, but his work in health and safety takes him into theatres and clubs quite often and I guess that it's there that he meets these actresses or, more truthfully, I suspect, 'actresses'. This one was called Samantha, as was the one before last, as I recall, and definitely one of the inverted commas variety.

I can't say that they were the happiest rehearsals I've ever known. It became clear quite quickly to everyone except George that Samantha was no Dame Judi. Speaking and moving at the same time seemed to be rather a challenge. And, as for the singing, well, Clive, our Musical Director, was in despair. He'd bang repeatedly on the right note, hoping that she would hit it or at least give it a passing wave as she slid by. She'd end up standing, hands on hips, yelling at him from the stage and poor Clive would sob quietly into his handkerchief.

And she could yell; she had a vocabulary that would make Billy Connolly blush. Clive resigned seven times in a fortnight. Always came back the next day; people will do anything to have an outlet for their creative talent. He said to me as we left one night, brushing what is left of his hair out of his eyes with the back of his hand, 'Simon, dear, I tell you, that madam will be the death of me. She sings "Someday My Prince Will Come" as if it's the "March of the Toreadors". Awful, though I must say I wouldn't mind, if we actually had a few toreadors prancing around.'

Not a ladies' man, our Clive.

I had a few run-ins with her myself. Problem was that she'd just go running to George. Or Squidgy, as she called him. Jilly and I had to keep a straight face about that one, the first time we heard it. And the second and the third. Actually, looking at what's happening to George's waistband, Squidgy's quite accurate. Though I don't think I'm man enough to tell him that juvenile leads are no longer his thing.

'Squidgy, sweetie,' she'd coo, 'I don't need to do that silly move that Simon's suggesting, do I? I mean, it will make me look stupid.'

'Nothing could make her look more stupid,' Jilly muttered to me as we withdrew, tails between our legs, to the back of the hall.

The trouble is that, basically, George finances these shows. With our audiences, we're never going to pay for all the props and costumes out of the box office. And he does like to strut his stuff in a lead role so, win/win, as the management consultants say. Until, of course, you disagree with him.

'Look, Simon, old chap,' he'd put his arm around my shoulder, 'Sam's a delicate flower but I think she has a real talent. Just cut her some slack, she'll come through, I'm sure. I'll give her some extra tuition, don't worry.' And he'd slap me on the back, assume I'd agreed, and be off. As far as I can see, Sam clearly does have a talent, but one that's more bed than boards.

Ros popped into rehearsals occasionally, sitting towards the back. She'd stay about half an hour, scribbling down notes for some reason. Then, with a grunt, she'd sail off again. She's a secretary of some kind, I believe. Quite high-flying, according to Jilly. I was hesitant about asking if she'd help with publicity as usual, but she volunteered like the trouper she is and was soon charging around the town putting up posters.

We staggered towards opening night and, through a combination of a lot of late nights and a good supporting cast, cobbled together a show that was not too embarrassing, if you closed your eyes at key moments. And your ears.

There was one particular moment at the end of the first act that did plumb the depths of the horror pit. Cinderella is left alone on stage for a final solo as she sits abandoned in her cellar. 'I Have a Dream', the Abba song. More a nightmare. Samantha just can't sing quietly. The first line would come out meandering drunkenly, barely within shouting distance of the tune, after which she'd resort to yelling out the words like a demented football fan. There was one night when Ros witnessed this. She caught my eye, raised a quizzical eyebrow and left the building. I tried to drop the song, but Samantha liked it; she'd been with her 'mates' thirteen times to Mamma Mia. So, Squidgy was brought into play and it was once again checkmate. I had decided that this scene would be a good time to slip out for a coffee on the first night.

Well, that first night came, inexorably, and the hall was quite full. Ros had done her work drumming up business, if anything better than usual. I couldn't help feeling that was a shame. Ros herself was nowhere to be seen. Unusual, as she likes to be on the door, supervising everything. Understandable, though, I suppose.

The curtain went up and we got through the first act. Only a couple of dries from Samantha, with some rather loud prompts from the curtains. Then the moment came for the song. I realised I was stuck, having left it too late to slip out, and sank down in my seat. Clive struck the opening chord, staring at his keyboard as if it was about to slide off the piano and make for the door. Perhaps that was what he was hoping.

As Samantha drew breath, the door at the rear of the hall burst open. Ros sailed in, resplendent in a full ballgown, strewn with pearls and topped with a tiara. She stood, like a large marquee, the light behind her. Then, as Sam gaped open-mouthed, Ros launched into the song. 'I have a dream, a fantasy'. The voice was gentle but melodic and somehow seemed to fill the entire hall. Clive sat bolt upright and immediately picked up the tune. Ros progressed up the aisle, a galleon in full sail, the voice growing clearer and even sweeter with every line. People started to sing and clap along. When she sang 'I believe in angels', I truly think half the hall agreed with her at that moment.

With perfect timing, she reached the stage on the last chorus, climbing the steps without missing a beat. As her final note faded, we were all on our feet applauding. All except Samantha, of course, who stomped off stage and into the night, where she belongs, closely pursued by Squidgy. No one noticed her absence, as Ros stood, taking her bows. Jilly appeared from the wings with the bouquet that we had reluctantly agreed to get for Samantha. I wished we had spent more. The cheering grew even louder as Ros received her flowers and wiped away a small tear.

We never got to the second act. Ros did five more numbers, which Clive seemed suspiciously well prepared for, and everyone went home very happy.

Next year, Ros as Dick Whittington. We'll find the money, somehow.

THE FLYER

Just before five on the afternoon of Saturday September 26th last year, my son Victor flew away. I had not seen him since that day, until tonight.

Do I blame myself? There's no value in thinking in terms of blame. Was I too single-minded, too hard a taskmaster? Science demands dedication if you are going to break through to anything worthwhile. And science is my first love, my god, you could say. All my life, nothing else mattered. Normal conversation is dull, holidays a bore and a waste of time. I have to keep my mind in focus; I have to chase the elusive, teasing solution.

People raise their eyebrows when I tell them of my field of endeavour. I have dedicated forty years to the study of man-powered flight. Why? Because I believe that it is the last great challenge left to us. Most find it frivolous. 'Isn't that just loonies dressed as chickens throwing themselves off the end of piers?' They are ignorant, don't understand. Imagine it. To fly like birds, in complete control of your destiny, soaring high, riding the thermals, looking down on the hills, the valleys and the ordinary, earthbound people below. This is the final frontier, our most noble quest.

It's not for me anymore, of course, not in any active sense. Age and one too many crashes have left me too immobile to attempt it again. Ironic, really, the one person who knows, really knows how to make a man fly, stuck in a wheelchair. That's why Victor was so important.

From when he was quite young, it was clear to me that he would be the one. Not for him a squandered youth. I would give him fame, immortality. Yes, it came at a price. I would occasionally see him looking out through the workshop window on a hot afternoon, watching the boys next door kicking a football around. I would simply remind him of the work to be done. And, later, girls would come to call. I would explain that Victor was too busy working with me on something important. Even the most persistent eventually gave up. That's the way it had been with my father and me and that's how it would be with him. My wife, of course, didn't understand it. She kept bleating on about rounded experience, growing up, being himself. She couldn't see how important this work was. After she left, it all became much more straightforward. Victor seemed to forget any stupid thoughts about wasting time and was constantly at my command. After my final accident, he became my arms and legs in all my work and, most importantly, my pilot. Sometimes I would wake him at two or three in the morning and get him to bring me some more writing paper or materials. Just to remind him of his role.

So many years of endless work, so many failures behind me. Yet I knew that each time, I was getting closer to the solution, to achieving that half-mile flight that would put me in the history books. The materials, the ratio of the wings to the body, the connection between man and equipment. Each time it became clearer and, by last September, I truly believed that I had achieved my goal.

Shortly after dawn on September 26th, we were on the flat top of a hill in Shropshire. This was the site of the main competition of the year. The decaying smell of late summer hung in the air. To the east, in the distance, I could see the white flag that marked the half-mile. Beyond the flag, the ground dropped away sharply. A light breeze came in from the north east, clearing the early autumnal mist. We don't fly with the wind; that's for hang-gliders and such dilettantes. You must fly across it, and I had worked out a way to use its lift indirectly, translating it into forward motion like the centreboard on a boat. Today, at last, it was going to work. I was sure of it.

We always arrived early but kept the equipment under wraps. I had devised a way of folding everything down so that it fitted into a large, elongated kit bag, away from prying eyes. We were scheduled to launch at three-thirty, which meant that we had to endure the usual array of idiots believing that an adapted bicycle and a few bits of string and cloth would achieve anything. Then there was the extra frustration of a couple of crashes demanding medical help and further delaying our launch time. At a quarter to five, the organisers came to us to say that they could not let us launch because of the fading light. Well, I was having none of it. The wind had freshened steadily during the afternoon and conditions were now ideal. I knew this was my moment.

Brushing them aside, I called to Victor and we unpacked the bag. Most of the other flyers and all of the press had gone, headed no doubt for the nearest pub, where they could swap tales of their absurd ideas and adventures. The few who were left watched like dumb animals as we assembled everything. Bosses slipped perfectly into their receiving sockets, sections clicked together and in five minutes, it stood complete, its broad wings gleaming in the late afternoon sun.

Victor stepped into the aerodynamic suit that I had designed. He turned to me with a slight, silly grin.

'Wish me luck, Dad.'

'It's not about luck. Now, quickly, before that wind drops.'

He gave me a look that I didn't understand at the time, then climbed into position. Because the officious fools running the event had ended the day's proceedings, they refused to wave us off. Victor looked back at me, confused.

'Go, for God's sake. Get on with it!' I shouted.

He put his head down and started to move forward. After about fifteen yards, I sensed a lift. Another twenty yards and he was airborne. He headed out on the ordained path, twenty foot above the ground and rising steadily. As I watched, all I could hear was the thunder of my own heartbeat. After three hundred yards, he was still airborne. I had come this far before, but no further. Four hundred, five hundred yards, and still aloft. He was barely visible in the evening light, just an occasional glint as the setting sun caught his wings. Six, seven, eight hundred yards and then it was past the flag that marked the half-mile. I had done it. I had created man-powered flight. The onlookers had now all gone and the organisers were busy with their paperwork; I was alone. I closed my eyes for a moment and leaned back in my chair.

When I opened them again, I could not see him. I searched methodically. I assumed he must have landed down in the valley. But then I seemed to glimpse a speck of light, rising up and up into the sky above us. A trick of the light? Probably.

I waited on that hill for an hour. I called the organisers and sent them running over to find him. They came back empty-handed. I sent them out again. Again, they came back with nothing. Suspecting a conspiracy, I insisted on a full search at first light the following morning. First a mile radius, then two and three miles. Nothing. Eventually, I went home.

And here I have stayed. There has been no award, no publicity. Because we flew after the meeting had officially finished, the pigmies of the organisation have refused to recognise my achievement. And the disappearance, while good tabloid fodder for a few days, made it hard to claim anything. None of that bothers me; I don't need the recognition of lesser scientists to know what I have achieved. It would have been nice for Victor, I concede, to have been famous but we don't always get what we want.

I just wish I knew where it was. And Victor, of course. Things don't just disappear; science does not allow such events. I don't like unsolved problems. During many sleepless nights, I have lain awake calculating the possible answers. Did Victor just continue in the direction he was heading? Did he crash somewhere and has simply not been found? Did he have a plan to steal the plane from me and keep it hidden? Was I betrayed by my own son? Unacceptable though that last thought was, I could think of no other solution. But then there was that light rising, soaring in the darkening sky. What was it? What had it meant?

Tonight, I was working late, as usual, trying some new variables. It was cold in the study, so I had wrapped a rug around my shoulders. Suddenly, I heard a movement behind me. I turned my chair and there was Victor, standing, silently looking down on me. My first feelings? Anger. Surprise. Irritation. All of these.

I was immediately full of questions. How far had he gone? Where was the kit? Was it in good condition? Had the struts held up under the pressure? Where the hell had he been for the last four months? 'For God's sake, answer me, where have you been?'

Victor just looked at me, a faint smile on his face. He turned to stare out of the study window. Eventually, his gaze fixed on me. He smiled broadly and said, 'Freedom'. Just that, just one word.

Nothing else. Just 'Freedom'. He left the room and walked out onto the lawn. I followed in the chair. He stood, looking up at the cloudless winter sky for a long time. Then he turned back, raised his hand in a kind of salutation, spread his arms out and just flew away. He just lifted off and flew away into the night. I watched him, anchored in silence to my chair, as he swooped over the trees, above the roof and away, out of sight.

This could not happen. Science forbade it. Yet, my own son had disproved my life's work. I felt the chill of the January night creep into me and, for the first time that I can remember, I wept. I let the rug fall from my shoulders. I will stay out here tonight. My work is over. There is nothing else to do. And, perhaps, in this way, I may be permitted to follow him.

AUNT ETHEL'S WAGGLE DANCE

Bees are clever little devils. It seems that, when they find a good pollen source, they buzz back to the hive, gather their chums together by spinning round in circles very fast then, pointing in the direction of said pollen, waggle their venomous little tushes with unseemly gusto. Everyone gets the message and off they all go for a damn good lunch. Apiarists, those fine, bearded, Morris-dancing men who dedicate themselves to the care of these fuzzy little creatures, call this the Waggle Dance.

Aunt Ethel was very like this. Not bearded, of course, that was Aunt Cicely, but prone to the waggle dance. I'm not suggesting for a moment that she looked like a bee. Tall, very tall, imagine Nelson's Column in a tight dress and fright wig. Kind people would have said that she had an aristocratic profile; those less filled with the milk of human kindness might have commented on nostrils that would have made a thoroughbred stallion boast. I think it was probably the nostrils that triggered her waggle dance. She could smell unattached wealth at fifty paces.

I was about seventeen when I first witnessed this performance. I'd come up to London during my last school holidays to spend some time with Aunt Ethel. 'See it as an extension of your education,' my mother had murmured with a look that hovered somewhere between challenge and pity, the one you adopt when you teach a dog to beg. And it was educational. Aunt Ethel took me off to the National Gallery to stand in silent homage before the Canalettos, to The Globe to stand in a light drizzle and be pulverised by Shakespeare's rhetoric and to Buckingham Palace to, well, stand and look at Buckingham Palace.

One afternoon, after returning from being made to feel inadequate by the Science Museum, we had collapsed into the very soft armchairs of her small Marylebone flat with tea and custard creams.

'Stephen, darling, I have to go to a do tonight,' she announced. 'Bit of a bore, probably, but you're welcome to come along.'

The alternatives of staying in with the television or going out to explore London on my own were greatly preferable but it was clearly one of those 'You don't have to if you don't want to' questions that expected the answer yes.

'Love to, Aunt. When do we leave?'

'About six-thirty. If we get there early, we can hoover up the snacks and then we won't have to bother with supper.' Aunt Ethel was not familiar with the ability of the seventeen-year-old male to eat every two hours and still feel the need to go scavenging. I pocketed a couple of biscuits.

Shortly before seven, we were at the door of an elegant house on the edge of Mayfair. This in itself surprised me. Aunt Ethel was always announcing to the world that she was but one step from destitution and a life on the streets, yet here we were in the best part of town. And she had dressed for the occasion, a long scarlet number with a couple of loops of pearls, hair swept back like an Afghan Hound in a high wind and make-up that could only be described as striking. I stood beside her in my one decent jacket, feeling like Oliver Twist just before that extra helpings episode.

The door opened at her knock and we were escorted up to the first floor, to a large room, all swathed curtains, chandeliers and hotel carpets.

'What is this do about?' I whispered to her.

'Oh, some charity thing,' she answered vaguely. 'A friend of mine asked me to come along.'

And with that she headed for the food table with the focused concentration of a tiger spying a tethered goat. She took up pole position by the vol-au-vents and sent me off for two glasses of 'something decent'. It took me a while to get back to her, as I was happily cornered by a redheaded girl from Albuquerque, whose 'paw' was Cultural Attaché at the American Embassy, which told me all I needed to know about American culture. By the time I had reluctantly made my excuses, woven my way across the now quite crowded room and returned to the feeding area, the plate of vol-au-vents in front of Aunt Ethel, as well as the smoked salmon sandwiches to the right and the chicken goujons to the left, had suffered serious damage. She had also contrived to already have a drink in her hand, a fact that did not stop her taking the one that I proffered. We both turned back to the food and I did my best to catch up. Then it happened.

Aunt Ethel's head jerked up. The nostrils flared; there is no other word, and it was a magnificent sight, up there with sunrise over Bali. She spun towards the door. With the advantage of height, she had a periscopic view over the heads of the assembled masses. She was focused on something, or someone, with radar-like intensity. And the waggle dance began. Glasses deposited on the table, her right hand went up to smooth her hair, then her left. Then the hands smoothed down her dress, and her body wiggled beneath its scarlet sheath like a bamboo in a hurricane. Her arms flexed, her neck flexed, her feet padded up and down and her hips rhumba-ed.

Then, after thirty seconds of this, she was off through the crowd like a purgative. I followed in her wake, casting my apologetic face towards several guests who were now suffering something akin to whiplash. I reached the door well behind her, in time to see her towering above a rather crumpled man who was pushing his glasses up his nose to get the top of her head in focus. A swing of Aunt Ethel's hips sent the elderly lady who had been escorting him out of range, she took him by the arm and led him towards the drinks.

At that point, small redhead from Albuquerque popped up again.

'So, you, like, live in the country. I guess that must mean, my Lord, that y'all are some kind of aristo or something.'

'More the something,' I muttered, watching Aunt Ethel's head weave through the crowd.

Redhead shrieked with laughter.

'My, I just love your English sense of humour. That's why I so like being here. You know,' she leaned in confidentially, 'back home they just don't do that, what do you call it, irony stuff. Back in Albuquerque, New Mexico, it's all tits and ass and chickens.'

I started to ask, I mean you would, wouldn't you, but her leaning in had not become leaning out. She was looking up at me, which was a change from the last few days. She had green eyes.

'Would you like some food?' I asked.

We wormed our way back across the room to the now depleted table, as I tried hard to remember if she was Cindy Jean or Candy Jane. She surveyed the pieces of curled sandwich and pastry crumbs very much the way I imagine Custer had surveyed his decimated army.

'Fancy going off and getting something to eat?' she purred.

My hesitation was not gentlemanly consideration but awareness that my schoolboy's allowance was not going to stretch to dinner in Mayfair.

'There's a place just around the corner,' she continued, green eyes sparkling, 'where I can pass the bill straight on to the embassy. Cool, huh?'

Cool indeed. Hesitation vanquished.

'Give me a minute to tell my aunt what's happening.'

'Sure. I'll see you by the door.'

I homed in on the rampant head of Aunt Ethel and made my way over. She had her hand on scruffy man's shoulder and was clearly explaining something to him. Scruffy man was nodding and giggling nervously.

I sidled up. 'Excuse me, Aunt.'

She didn't hear, or at least didn't acknowledge. I repeated the greeting. She paused in mid-sentence and slowly turned towards me. For a moment, I could see her struggling to remember who I was. Then the lights came on.

'Ah, Stephen, meet Cecil. He owns Leicestershire.'

'Lincolnshire, actually,' he giggled. 'And not all of it. Not really. Actually.'

'Cecil, this is my nephew, Stephen. My sister is much older than me. Stephen is going to Oxford.'

'Oxford? Really? Gosh, well, that's yes, um well … Oxford,' and he gave a whistling sigh like a deflating balloon.

'Yes, thank you,' I managed. 'Aunt, I'm just going to pop out for a bite to eat. With, er, that person over there.'

I pointed vaguely towards the door. Her reply was equally vague.

'Good, fine. See you later. You have a key?'

'Yes.'

'Fine, bye.' This last bit was over her shoulder as she refocused on Cecil.

It didn't last, of course. Neither of the trysts of that evening. Clarrie Jo, as it turned out, and I had a happy, bouncy few weeks before her father pointed out that Cultural Attaché at the American Embassy actually meant spy, with all the equipment that came with it, and if I continued to do that to his daughter, he would share some interesting techniques with me. Aunt Ethel did a bit better. She and Scruffy Cecil were an item long enough for him to share the spoils of Lincolnshire with her. She now has a very nice apartment in Nice and can be seen at all the best parties. Still on the lookout, still waggle dancing.

CHARLIE AND THE LADY

Charlie was sixteen and as skinny as a broomstick when he ran away from home. Well, fifteen and ten months, to be exact, though there was little point in being exact. His mother, who gazed vaguely at life from the wrong side of a conveyor belt of own label vodka, was never that sure when his birthday was anyway. It seemed to wander between May and August each year. One day his mother would shake him awake and announce, 'Happy Birthday, darling' and he would know that it would be one of those days when she would laugh loudly at everything that was said, while the tears made mascara rivulets down her cheeks.

He'd felt bad about leaving her. But, in the end, it came down to survival. Her latest 'gentleman friend', neither friend nor gentleman, had decided that Charlie needed to be taught a lesson, get some discipline knocked into him. Two lost teeth and a fractured arm later, Charlie packed as many clothes as he could into his school backpack, stirred a double dose of laxative into the man's evening tea, and, while he was otherwise engaged, emptied his wallet and left the house forever.

Two hundred miles away and four nights sleeping rough in the cold April air had him longing for his bed. What money he had left was stolen by an ex-sailor who had promised to show him the ropes. Charlie found himself standing by some waste ground, known in council-speak as the Recreation Park, watching a group of kids kick a football around. He had spent the previous night in a nearby builder's yard, crunched up in one of a row of Portaloos, and was wondering if he would ever lose the smell of industrial strength disinfectant. He looked up to see a tattered poster flapping on the window of an empty shop.

Gueppo's Circus, coming your way!!!

He checked the date. Today. Wrapping his parka around him, he waited.

By eleven o'clock, there were men, big men everywhere, pulling on ropes, hammering pegs, shoving caravans into place. Charlie approached the nearest, who was swinging a mallet, tattooed muscles bulging out of a stained black t-shirt.

'Any chance of work?' he asked, shyly.

The man looked up and down Charlie's huddled frame and grinned. 'Sorry, kid, candy floss machine is already manned.' An accent Charlie didn't recognise.

He nodded and started to walk away.

'Hey. You give up that easy, you really going to starve. Over there, see that guy with beard and silver jacket. The one doing fuck-all? That's boss. Go ask him. And try to look more bloody cheerful. And bigger.'

With a laugh at his own joke, which Charlie did his best to copy, he swung the mallet again. Charlie walked across the rough ground to the bearded man, who was shouting at an official-looking person in a suit.

'Listen, mate, I told you, the toilets will be here by one.' The harsh cockney accent was almost reassuring to Charlie. 'Then you'll be able to put a tick in your little box and everyone will be happy. OK?'

The suited man tucked his forms into his briefcase.

'I'll be back at two. No toilets, no show.'

'Don't worry, they'll be here.'

As the official walked away, the owner turned to Charlie.

'You local?'

Charlie nodded. If you didn't say the words, it's not really a lie, is it?

'Know where I can find twenty toilets in two hours, keep that wanker off my back?'

'There's a builder's yard round the corner. They've got some.'

The man set off at a pace. Charlie stood watching him walk away, and, with him, any hope of a job. After a few paces, the man turned back.

'Come on, then, I'm not going to find it on my own in this one-shit town.'

An hour later, the toilets were booked, and Charlie had a job. Well, at least, he had somewhere to sleep and a couple of meals a day. For that, he ran errands, helped with the box office, cleaned the toilets, basically everything that the others didn't want to do. He slept in a small space on the end of the lions' cages. He didn't sleep well.

Over the next few days, as they moved on, Charlie soon found out that circus people were not the cheerful, jolly folk of storybooks. The circus was a nowhere land for anyone who didn't want to exist on any official record. Criminals, illegal immigrants, child molesters, bankrupts, they all had a reason to disappear into this rough and rootless life. Once again, he found himself on the receiving end of the punches. Any time he dropped something, got in the way or even sat eating his food, a cuff over the head would come from nowhere. The clowns were the worst – vicious, unsmiling, working in a gang to grind down anyone who looked vulnerable. Right now, Charlie knew he had no choice, but he checked the window of the Job Centre in every town they visited to find the way out.

One evening in a Somerset town, after the audience had been sent happily away and Charlie was heading for bed, he found himself cornered behind the animal cages by three of the clowns.

'So, pretty boy, what you going to do for us? You got a little dance for Georgie?'

'You want us to show you what that pretty arse of yours is really for?'

Charlie looked around desperately, trying to find a way out. There was none.

The three men closed in on him.

'Leave him.'

The voice, quiet and low, came from behind them. They spun round. Into their midst walked Matilda. The men backed off. No one messed with Matilda, four foot two of muscle and frown and a fearless bareback rider. What she lacked in size, she made up for in radiated menace. Even Charlie had heard the story of Samson, the Albanian strongman, who had two-timed her with one of the acrobats. She had cut off more than his hair.

She glared around.

'Anyone touches the kid answers to me.'

'Hey, Matilda, we was just having a bit of fun.'

One look silenced them.

'Go.'

They went.

She turned to Charlie.

'You, follow me.'

Charlie mutely followed to her caravan.

It was two days before he came out again, two days that he would remember for the rest of his life; the rich, musky smell of the caravan; drinking Diamond White cider; Dylan's *Bringing It All Back Home*, over and over, the only tape she had; and Matilda's green eyes gazing at him and through him.

But even that was not enough to keep him. A month later, he answered an ad that he saw in the Job Centre in Ramsgate for a trainee salesman. He cried when he told Matilda he'd been accepted. She just stared hard at him and muttered in her gruff voice, 'You must leave now, take what you want, you think will last, but whatever you want to take, you'd better grab it fast.'

She meant it. Two minutes later, she burned his parka.

ANNIVERSARY

He stands at the side of the road. An old man, shivering, ducking away from the harsh light of the street lamp, as if it might somehow damage him, letting it splash off the crumpled snow. His gaze does not move from the lighted window opposite. Hazy through the mist on the glass, a tall Christmas tree, illuminated by the glow of a television. Solitary and ignored, it twinkles at him in silent conspiracy. He smiles back.

'Look, Maisie,' he whispers. 'Look. I bet little Jack's getting really excited. He'll be longing to pick up that parcel and shake it. And Jenny'll be fussing away, trying to find out if we've got her that doll.' A laugh burst from him, shaking his slight frame. 'Took me four hours to find that blessed thing. And then a blooming air raid warning just as I was paying. They flew over anyway, came out this way, didn't they? What a night to choose for a raid, eh, Maisie? Christmas Eve. Bastards.' His face clouds over for a moment, then the smile returns. 'Pardon the language, my dear. And then fighting back home through the blackout. Still, a lot better than being out in North Africa, eh?' Shivering again, he makes to pull his coat around him. To his surprise, it isn't there. He spreads his arms.

'Look at me, Maisie, thinking it's high summer. I must be … Is that turkey trussed and ready, then? I was thinking about that all the way back. Came from Fred down at The Feathers. Best bit of black-market bird I could find, eh. Blooming bus took hours. Lord knows how the driver found his way. No lights, no road signs, nothing. Daft, really. As if a spy's going to attack us by bus.' He peers up into the sky. 'Bomber's moon. That's what they say, isn't it, Maisie. So how come they were so bloody inaccurate, then. I mean, we're miles from the factories. I was so excited, though, as I walked that last mile from the stop. Couldn't wait to show you what I'd got. Though I have to admit, when I saw Charlie coming down the street, I was tempted to pop into The Queen's Head with him for a quick pint. Felt I deserved it, I suppose. But then I could tell. Something stopped me. Even in the pitch dark. There was something about the way he was walking. Kind of slow and heavy. I just stood, waiting for him to come up to me.'

The old man looks down at the ground, not noticing that his carpet slippers are sodden. 'Do you know what he said to me? Weird, really. He said, "The kids are OK, Joe. The kids are OK." I didn't know what he meant. Or didn't want to know, I suppose. I started to make some silly joke about Christmas puddings or something. Then he started to tell me about the bombs in the High Street and, well, about you, Maisie. God help me, love, I swore at him, called him the most terrible things, f-ing liar and worse. I won't repeat to you what I said, but it was not nice. I even thumped him. I'm so ashamed about that, I know how you don't like that sort of thing, Maisie. But, good old Charlie, he just put his arm round my shoulder and led me off. I can't remember where to. But there were the kids sitting very still, just sort of staring. Someone had given them some cocoa, but it had gone cold, got that skin on it. The police station. It must have been the police station. Yes, that's right. The police station. I'll show you the doll. I've got it … Now, where did I leave it?'

The door to the house opposite opens and a man in his sixties comes out, wearing a paper hat on his balding head. 'Dad,' he calls, 'Dad, what the hell are you doing? We've been looking for you everywhere.' He comes quickly down the path and across the road. 'Come on, you daft old man. You'll catch your death.' He stops opposite his father, hands on hips.

'I'm sorry, Jack. It's just… We were chatting… Your mother… Sort of anniversary, I suppose.'

The man looks down at his father, at the tears spilling from his reddened eyes. 'OK, Dad. Come on in. Come on. I'll make you a nice warm drink.' And he puts his arms round the old man's sloping shoulders and leads him gently back inside the warm house.

THE ART OF BEING HAPPILY MARRIED

Some people, most of us, in fact, are simply married. We don't make a big deal about it, everyone gets it. It doesn't need hammering home. Suzy and Charles were different. They were A Couple. They carried their togetherness around like a megaphone. We were all endlessly subjected to their constant gasps of amazement that God had been wise enough to grant each to the other. And, while most of us keep nicknames to the bedroom, we had to dig up the indulgent smile when we heard all about Sozzlekins and Chucklebuns. And, on the subject of bedrooms, Suzy was clear to a fault about Charles' prowess in that department. Clear to an indigestible fault. All right for teenage conversation, perhaps, but these two were well into their thirties.

Which makes it all the harder to explain what happened last Saturday. Saturday's routine for Paula and me is usually a mix of insufficient lie-in, rushing round shops, then quick trip to the pub as a reward. Not quite so normal this time. Paula had had a busy week, late-night meetings and so on. She'd lost a string of pearls and was making a big fuss about it before we went out. I do remember getting them for her, actually, quite nice, though couldn't really recall what they looked like. Never been very good at remembering that sort of thing. So, the fact they were missing was obviously my fault. Anyway, we were hunting around, then she suddenly said, 'Oh, forget it, let's get the shopping done,' and that was that.

It was sunny when we got to the pub, one of the first warm ones of the year, warm without that back bite of chill that so often catches the over-optimistic outdoor drinker, leaving him shivering into his beer. After our little morning contretemps, we'd managed to finish the Sainsbury's purgatory faster than usual and were well settled at a table out front, just by the door, with our dry white wine and pint of Old Peculier. So, as it turned out, well positioned to watch the ensuing three-act opera.

Suzy and Charles normally arrive gropingly intertwined like unruly clematis but today, as they came down the road, we could immediately detect a certain froideur. There was at least a six-inch gap between them; we could see daylight.

'We'll sit out here, Charles, with Paula and Johnny.' It was an instruction.

'I think it's a bit chilly. We'd be better inside.'

'No.'

Charles hesitated. There was some battle going on inside his head and he was clearly on the losing side.

Finally, he muttered, 'OK, I'll get you a drink,' and slunk, yes, slunk into the pub. Extraordinary. No Bunnykins, no Sugar Plumlet, they were speaking to each other like, well, like the rest of us lesser mortals speak to each other. This was a shock equal to being told that Father Christmas did not exist.

Suzy slumped onto the bench opposite us.

'Lovely day, Suzy.'

A quivering smile, straight out of *Bambi*.

'Everything OK?' asked Paula, with that way women have of combining concern and triumph in one simple question.

'Oh, you know,' muttered Suzy and waited for us to press her further. Paula pressed.

'You look a bit out of sorts, sweetie.'

'Well, it hasn't been the best of mornings,' Suzy leaned forward conspiratorially, blood coming out of the stone with surprising ease. She glanced towards the pub door. 'Charles thinks I'm getting old.'

The lip quiver returned, eyes widened and moistened till she looked like that cat in *Shrek*. Now, these two are a good five years younger than us, so mention of age is definitely thin-ice territory. At least, it is for Paula, who cares more about these things. Women do, it seems.

'Really?' There was a razor-sharp edge to Paula's reply, a Queen of Hearts off with their heads tone that I had become increasingly familiar with recently. I tried to send a telepathic 'change the subject' message to Suzy but frankly she only has two brain cells, and they were both switched to transmit.

'Yes, I'd just got back from two hellish days in Birmingham and was feeling pretty wiped out and he goes and gives me a present that just reeks of middle age. I mean, how would you feel about that, Paula. I mean, I know you're older, well, a bit older than me and, well, you do dress in a way that's, maybe, a little more conservative but would you, I mean, even you be grateful for ... '

Suzy paused, clearly confused as to why she was now talking to a very blank and icy wall. Fortunately, Charles reappeared with their drinks.

'Ah, Charles,' I cried, 'Watching the rugby later?'

'Certainly am,' he replied, clearly grateful to talk about anything that dwelt in a world independent of him and Suzy. 'Don't fancy England's chances, though, sadly.'

We bantered on for a couple of minutes, but I could see out of the corner of my eye that Suzy was not done yet. Finally, inevitably, as we were men and not built for words, our conversation dried up.

Suzy pounced on the silence.

'Paula, does Johnny buy you presents that you're glad to have?'

'Yes, of course, because he always buys me exactly what I tell him to buy.'

'And is he good at hiding them from you?'

Paula's brow furrowed, not sure where this was going. I certainly couldn't enlighten her. 'Yes, he always hides them in his sock drawer.'

This caught me out. I thought I was particularly adept at the hiding thing.

Charles cut across his wife's flow.

'Suzy, honey, they don't want to hear about our little problems.'

Even I could detect a note of desperation. Must have been a major boo-boo, whatever it was. One advantage of being totally uninventive in the present department and just taking orders is that I never get something inappropriate.

Suzy treated us to a smile of false radiance worthy of a shampoo ad.

'It's OK, Charles,' her voice rising half an octave, as if talking to a retarded four-year-old. 'I just want to check if I'm being unreasonable.'

'Well, we don't wash our dirty linen, do we?'

I could see Paula hovering between doing the right thing and pure nosiness. Nosiness won, of course; it always does.

'Look, Suzy, if we can help at all.'

'Suzy,' Charles' voice was getting higher. I had the impression that someone was squeezing him where you don't want to be squeezed. 'I really don't think it's anyone else's business. Now, please ...'

Suzy looked steadily at him as if she was deciding whether to eat him for supper or scrape him into the waste bin. Then she turned back to Paula.

'Paula, if you got a present, would you expect to find it shoved under your side of the bed, no box, no wrapping, nothing?'

Paula seemed to be going pale. Maybe it was a bit cold out here. She stared across at Charles. Sending him a sympathy message, I supposed. Then she turned back to Suzy and silently shook her head.

'And,' Suzy's voice rose to a triumphant crescendo, 'would you expect that present to be the ultimate old person's consolation prize, a pearl necklace?'

'Actually, Suzy,' I jumped in, 'pearls are very flattering and not a bit fuddy-duddy. In fact, I got some for Paula ...'

It was my turn to stare. I was staring at Suzy, sitting arms spread and one of those of course I'm right looks on her face. I felt rather than saw the look that passed between Paula and Charles.

We all went home pretty quickly after that.

Paula and I are not talking.

OLD HABITS

'Haven't seen you round here before.'

The soft, female voice makes him look up, surprised, alert. A moment ago, the pub had been empty. Where had she appeared from? But, straight away, the old habits kick in. He grins the much practised grin that, combined with a steady look straight into her eyes, forms the overture to a consistently successful performance.

'No,' he keeps his voice low and conspiratorial, 'this is new for me.' He looks out of the pub window to the late afternoon light playing on the walls of the small harbour. 'I just needed to get away for a while.'

'Away? Away from what, if you don't mind me asking.'

He feels the familiar adrenaline rush. So easy. He motions to her to sit down.

'It's been a rather traumatic time recently,' he murmurs, pausing as she leans in, eyes wide with anticipation. 'You see, my wife, well, she died rather tragically in April. I just needed to be somewhere different for a while.' He returns his gaze from the window to her face. 'I'm sure you understand.'

'You poor thing.' She gazes back.

He is surprised to feel a small twinge of guilt, an echo deep within him. After so long, and so many times, his mother's Puritan voice. *No good will come of this, mark my words.* As always, as he did so often when Susie was still alive, he pushes it quickly aside.

He sighs heavily, stares at the table. 'Yes, terrible thing. She just drove off one morning and that was the last time I saw her. Hit a tree. Gone.' No mention of the row, the tears, the threats before the door slammed. No mention of the coroner's suspicion of suicide. Why muddy a good story?

He sees the girl's eyes glisten and leans forward.

'Sorry, didn't mean to upset you. I'm Gerry, by the way.' He reaches a hand forward.

'Angie.'

She takes his hand. He holds the grip a moment longer than necessary. She notices and smiles.

'So,' he brightens his voice, 'what's there to do around here?'

She laughs. 'Not that much. There's quite a nice restaurant along the beach and the walk on the clifftop can be spectacular, especially towards sunset. But that's about it.'

'That sounds enough for me, the way I am at the moment.' Walk, dinner, bed, he thinks. It's all falling into place nicely. Sleeping alone is so dull. 'I think I'll try the walk; the fresh air will do me good. Look,' carefully timed hesitation, 'would you, I mean, how about joining me for the walk? You could show me the best views.'

She shrugs. 'Sure. I've nothing on for the rest of the day. Why not.'

Nothing on, he thinks. Yes, please.

'That's very kind. Shall we?'

As they leave the bar, the landlord walks through from the other room. He seems to give them a strange look. Jealousy, Gerry thinks. Always the way.

The path up from the harbour is steep and he takes every opportunity to offer Angie a hand. By the time they reach the top, the sun is starting to settle towards the sea, spreading its rays. They pause where the path comes close to the edge of the cliff. As he stands and looks out, he sees the colours change, deepening, becoming richer as they spread across the surface of the water. He feels a calm that has evaded him for so many years, a realisation that it is not all about winning, about defeating, hunting down and destroying. He feels an overwhelming urge to drop the game, the pretending and just be.

'It's quite something,' he says. 'I'm really glad you were able to show this to me.'

'Me too. So, does this make you feel any better?'

'It does. And so do you, you know. You seem to know what I need.'

Angie looks out across the sea, her head to one side. He finds the stance slightly disconcerting, can't think why. He looks at her hair blowing softly across her face, at the curves of her body. The old rush soars back, a beating in his head, right through his very being. He can feel her body under his, hear her murmurs and cries. One last time, maybe, he thinks, one more before kicking the habit.

After a while, she speaks again.

'Do you ever wonder why your wife died?'

'Why? No. As I said, car crash, just one of those things.'

'Just one of those things. Yes. No, I only ask because accidents are so often not just accidents.'

Gerry feels the beginnings of annoyance. This is not going according to the plan.

'Well this one was. Just an accident. I really don't want to talk about it.'

Angie turns towards him.

'No, I'm sure you don't. Just as you don't want to talk about the other women.'

'Other women? What other women? I can assure you …'

'Well, the secretary in the accounts department, that woman you met at the annual conference, Jim's wife – as in Jim, your best man, in case you've forgotten that one – the waitress when you and Susie were on holiday in Crete. And oh, so many more, but I don't need to go on, do I?'

He stares, open-mouthed.

'How do you know this? Have you been spying on me? Who put you up to this? Who the hell are you?'

'Who the hell am I?' She laughs loudly. Gerry looks away, back down the path, searching for an escape. 'Who am I? Look closely, Gerry.' She grabs his lapel, forcing him round to face her. 'Look very closely.'

As he turns to stare at her, her face slowly changes. In place of the soft, pretty features of Angie, his horrified eyes are looking at Susie, a bruised, battered, blood-spattered Susie.

He screams. He doesn't see her arm swing round, but he feels the blow that sends him stumbling towards the cliff edge. It is the last thing he feels.

The coroner's verdict is suicide.

LADIES WITH SENSIBLE SHOES

The first thing that he noticed about the two elderly ladies, beside the rather astonishing fact that they seemed to know him, was that they were wearing very sensible shoes; flat, sturdy, laced up, the sort of shoes that people used to wear back then, out there.

George prided himself on his powers of observation, frequently finding the opportunity to demonstrate this to his staff at MCC, the Ministry of Communication Control. A tell-tale anachronism in a bulletin that had to appear current; the wrong-coloured badge; someone drinking one more coffee than their quota; all picked up with relish.

That morning had started well. The personal infotab set into his left earlobe woke him with a reassuringly bland news update and gave him his appointments for the day. The tab was tailored to exclude all unnecessary news such as sport and celebrity gossip. George, in his position as a Grade Seven Manager in the Ministry, wrote the news and was well aware that most televised sport did not actually happen nowadays, but was just composites of earlier games. And celebrities had all been avatars for years, ever since that embarrassing episode when the elderly Sir David Beckham had become confused and had accidentally denounced the President.

George's kitchen had, as always, greeted him warmly and responded instantly to his demand for tea, toast shade six and berry-ish jam. This was how he liked it, everything working smoothly, no mess. Breakfast was quickly consumed without thought or expectation. Checking in the mirror that his blue ministry overall, fresh each morning, was perfectly symmetrical, he stepped out into the corridor. The ladies were passing at that moment. He had never seen them before and was puzzled about how they had obtained access to the sixty-seventh floor of a restricted Gov Dom building. He was about to challenge them when they smiled at him and, in unison, said a cheery 'Good morning, Mr Jackson.'

Confused, George grunted a reply and stepped into the lift, which had registered his door opening and now stood ready for him. He descended to the garage on the twentieth floor and straight into his personal transporter. He sat back and barked 'Office'. The door slid shut and he was whisked away onto the sky road.

He normally checked the news channels as he glided on his fourteen-minute journey along the magnetic beam highway. But those ladies had unsettled him. And those shoes. He looked down at his own soft, brushed suede-ish pair for reassurance. None came. He stared out, looking without interest at the tops of buildings flashing by. As his transporter swung nearer the edge to pass another, he could see down into the world below. He remembered immediately why MCC advised people not to look down.

'Don't look down, it'll give you a frown
Look up and along and you'll be on song'.

One of our better slogans, mused George. Below, in the grey half-light, he could make out the rusting wrecks of ancient cars, immobile for years since the final great gridlock. Figures scurried between them, huddled, George guessed, against the cold. They crouched in the spaces where doors to the buildings had been before all of the doors were permanently sealed. Beyond them the city seemed to stretch forever. He was glad he was on the inside.

The day did not go particularly well for George. He found it hard to concentrate and was aware of the raised eyebrows of his Grade Eight bosses. He was in charge of the team that were creating next week's news. To his horror, he found at one point that he had put in the same item about a victory over the

Americans on two consecutive days. It was as if those shoes were marching behind him through the day, taunting him. He was quite relieved when the transporter swooped him into his bay at seventeen forty-three as usual late that afternoon. The lift was waiting, and he was quickly being whisked reassuringly to his sixty-seventh floor.

Leaving the lift, he walked up the corridor to his flat, gave the voice recognition command and strode in through the opening door. Instantly, a smell, sweet and musty, wrapped itself around him like a warm scented towel. A second later he realised that he was not alone. In the kitchen, his kitchen, busying themselves with equipment that George knew was not his, were the two elderly ladies. One of them, a stocky woman with close-cut grey hair, looked up.

'Oh, hello, dear. Right on time.'

George stood, mouth open, emitting little mewing noises, struggling to deal with the first break in his routine for twenty-three years. The ladies moved purposefully around the kitchen, which was strewn with white powder, splashes of liquid and strange gooey lumps.

'Kylie, dear,' said the first to her more willowy colleague, 'I think they will be ready now. Could you check, please, while I lay the table for George?'

The taller lady, Kylie, picked up a thick glove and opened the door of a large metal box that was sitting on George's usually pristine kitchen table. As the door opened, there was a blast of hot air and the smell intensified tenfold. She withdrew a black tray on which stood circular, bread-like shapes, each some three centimetres high and rough in texture.

She prodded one with a knife. 'Perfect, I believe, Mel, dear,' she said with a triumphant smile.

George found his voice. 'What on earth do you think you are doing here?' The authority that he had hoped his voice would carry was entirely missing.

'Why, dear, we're making you tea,' replied Kylie, not even looking up from her work.

'If I want tea, I have simply to ask my kitchen for it. I do not need anyone's help,' replied George. He sensed vaguely how stuffy he must sound, but that was subsumed by the struggle to understand why he was engaging in a conversation about tea with two strangers who had broken into his flat.

'I'm afraid not,' said Mel. 'You see, dear, we had to disconnect this bizarre and incompetent thing you call a kitchen so that we could set up our equipment. And please do not mistake the thin, grey liquid that it gives you for a cup of tea. Two very different things, as you are about to discover. Now wash your hands and sit down, dear, before it gets cold.'

George, obeying a deeply learned childhood reaction, did as he was told. Kylie put a plate in front of him. George looked at the plate. It was beautifully patterned, blue and white, depicting some kind of scene in a Chinese garden with people crossing a bridge. And it was made of a hard material, very different from the usual bendy disposables. Beside it was a knife, but this one was silver, shiny and, as George found when he picked it up, heavy.

'Have a scone, dear,' said Mel. 'Let me prepare it for you. I'm guessing that you have never seen one of these.' George silently shook his head.

Deftly, Mel split the scone horizontally. A wisp of steam rose from its pitted surface. She spread some thick yellow substance and then added something that looked to George like jam, except that it was lumpy, irregular and much thicker than his usual.

'Eat,' she commanded, and George obediently reached out. It occurred to him, briefly, that he might be about to be poisoned but the cacophony of aromas that attacked his nostrils was irresistible.

He bit into the loaded scone. Tastes exploded in his mouth, textures fought and blended. He was tasting a whole new world in one instant. His hands waved in vague circles, his head lolled back, tears sprang to his eyes. He would have declared that it was better than sex if he had ever had sex and if he had not been sitting with two respectable elderly ladies. He looked up at the two, who were standing, beaming at him.

'What is this? It's fantastic!'

'It's food, dear. Real food. Now, you must have a cup of tea.' Kylie picked up a round pot with a handle at one end and a sort of curved spout at the other and held it over a cup with the same pattern as the plate, but of a more delicate material, tapered and seated on a small plate of its own. She tipped the pot and a stream of clear, golden brown liquid poured into the cup. She added some milk, stirred and passed it to George. He took a sip. Each part of his mouth picked up a different taste. It was as if he had been transported to the temples and mountains of India, not that George had ever travelled beyond the reach of the sky road around the city, but he had seen pictures.

'This is just … just wonderful,' gasped George, reaching for another piece of scone. 'But who are you and what are you doing here, in my flat?'

'I'm so sorry, dear, how terribly rude of us. My name is Mel Dawson-Evans, and this is my good friend Kylie Macpherson. Oh, and we are urban terrorists. Do have some more jam with that, dear. It's terribly good, we made it ourselves.'

George froze, the scone half into his mouth. Very, very reluctantly, he put it down.

'Urban terrorists?' he gasped.

Mel giggled, rather embarrassed. 'Yes, dear. It does sound a bit melodramatic, doesn't it? But I think that, on balance, it is the best way to describe us.'

George blinked. He had written many stories about the dangers of urban terrorists, infiltrators from out there. The stories had always followed strict guidelines sent down from above and had always been checked before broadcast. Often, upstairs had added some more lurid details to his drafts. Urban terrorists were dangerous, ruthless and disease-ridden, dirty, rat-faced men who crept through the sewers at night to attack honest civilians.

'Does this mean that you're here to kill me?'

Both ladies burst into peals of laughter. 'Good heavens, no, dear. What would be the point of that? No, we are here to convert you.'

'Convert me to what?'

'To interconnectedness. In Here with Out There.'

George paled. He knew that out there was wretched, dangerous, a forbidden place of cold, hunger and shadows. The Great Threat. He shared this view with the ladies.

'Do have some more scone, dear,' said Mel. 'Does this look like the produce of hunger and cold? Do we?' George looked at them properly for the first time. Both stood upright, exuding good health, their faces brown in a way that sun lamps never achieved. Their clothes were made of materials that seemed softer than any of the man-made fibres of George's world.

'I don't understand,' he admitted.

'No, of course you don't. How could you. You see, George, you've never been told about the land beyond the city. There are places there where real food grows, where we can get the best from all over the world. Your people here, the gang of that awful little President,' George winced at such blasphemy, especially the 'little'. No one was permitted to mention the height of the

President, may the powers protect him. 'They don't want you to know about it but it's true. Here, look at these.' So saying, Mel spread out some photographs. George saw vast fields full of crops, herds of cows, people sitting down at long tables piled with food of all shapes and sizes.

'But why me?'

'Oh, it's not just you, dear. We and our friends are visiting hundreds of people. That's why I say we are urban terrorists, you see. We are going to overthrow this rather nasty regime, but we're going to do it with scones, not guns. Rather clever, really, don't you think?'

George blinked. 'But how will you overthrow the President, may the powers protect him, and why?'

Mel sighed. 'Oh, George, you really do have a long way to come. I thought you'd be a bit brighter, working as you do for the Ministry of Communication Control.' She waved away George's astonished question. 'How do we know where you work? The same way we know how to get into your flat and disarm your dreadful kitchen. We are very well informed, George. Each new recruit tells us who to approach next. And you can be very useful to the cause, George, in such an influential position. Now, have another scone and another cup of tea while we tidy up.'

'So, what do you expect of me?' asked George between bites and gulps.

'Oh, nothing, dear. We will pop in occasionally and give you another meal, just to keep you interested. Perhaps a nice beef stew next; Kylie has a wonderful recipe. Then, when there's enough of us, we'll just take over. And we can all get on with a much better way of life. That be nice, won't it. Anyway, must rush, dear. We'll leave you to tidy up if you don't mind. We have to get on to our next date.'

And with that, they gathered up their equipment and their portable oven and were gone, leaving George, to his great delight, with the remaining scones, butter and jam. He sat, staring at the disorderly kitchen, so different from the textbook tidiness that he had left just hours before. His eyes fell again to the scones and he reached for the knife.

'Ah,' he thought, as he started to butter another one. 'Interconnectedness. That explains the sensible shoes.'

JACK

If I sit very, very quietly, I can hear the worms under the lawn. I sit for a really long time listening. It's like when the television's on. I can hear the wires and tubes and things and they're more interesting to me than what's happening on the screen.

And when my mum shouts at me, 'Why are you just staring at the wall?' Well, I'm not. I'm listening to sounds and smelling smells and looking at the shapes in the wall, connecting the patterns and making new shapes. But I can't tell her that because she's not in my world. So we end up staring at each other. She usually cries then, and I watch the tears run down her face to see which way they will go, and which gets to the bottom of her face first.

When we go out, people look at me and then look away and then look at me again. I just look back. Faces are all different shapes and they all have funny expressions, like a mixture of laughter and a sort of dislike.

When Dad comes home, he comes up to see me and picks me up and throws me up in the air. He talks to me about the day and says things like, 'This is a secret, Jack, but if anyone can keep a secret it's you, you poor sod,' and then he'll tell me about someone called Claudia that he's been with. It's good when he throws me around. I can see things from different angles. And then Dad will say something like 'Oh, what the hell,' and go back downstairs to Mum.

Sometimes I shout out loud for a long time. Mum and Dad keep saying 'What's the matter?' but nothing's the matter really. It's just that I'm shouting. It echoes in my head and makes my arms and legs tingle.

Of course, the thing that I can hear most clearly is my own body. I can hear the blood going round the veins and that nice squeaky noise that the muscles make when you move them. Sometimes I just concentrate on one bit, like my toes, and it's like I can talk to my bones. It's probably because I can't move much; that helps me hear all those things. I can hear how it's all slowing down, too. Mum and Dad keep taking me to the doctors. They prod me and put things on me and then they talk quietly together. I don't think they know that I can hear. The word 'degenerative' comes up a lot. I think that means that I'll die soon. I wonder what that will sound like.

I've just come downstairs. I don't do that very often because it takes quite a long time. I hadn't seen Mum for a while and wondered where she was. Mum is lying on the kitchen floor, very still. There's something on the table, a bottle, some white things, pills probably, but they aren't making any noises. I listen to Mum carefully, but I can't hear her blood swishing round her. That must be what it's like when you stop. It looks quite calm. I think I'll like that.

DANCE LIKE NOBODY'S WATCHING

Edward Smith. God, he hates that name. Typical of his parents to give him something so pompous, so boringly old English and safe. This is 1967 after all, Britain is the coolest place on earth, the fulcrum of the Summer of Love, though that seems to pass by Edward, and the whole of Nuneaton, for that matter. Now more like the Autumn of Desperation. The world is full of Clints, Storms, Rorys and Ringos. Name a pop star called Edward. Anyway, the full name's only ever used by his mum or teachers, usually with that rising note that somehow crams impatience, disapproval, exasperation and general world-weariness into two syllables.

He steps out from under the bus shelter and puts his face up to the evening rain. There's that brief moment, when the rain first hits him, that's fantastic. He feels like he's part of it, part of the whole nature thing. Then it starts to drip down the collar of his school shirt and he's just wet and cold.

He's tried every version. Eddie, too queer; Ted, the sort of name decrepit and slightly creepy great-uncles have; Ed, more a past tense than a name. And that's not counting the versions his family come up with. 'Go, Teddy Boy,' his dad would call out across the school playing field. Crawl into a hole moment. And, worst of all, from Gran. He feels his insides shrink at the memory. 'How's my little Teddy-Weddy Bear?' It's just recently that he's realised that she only says that when his friends are around. Weird woman, his gran. Must be the endless cups of thick black tea she gets through. Pickled her brain. That or the Bourbon biscuits.

'Hey, Edo,' the voice comes from the other side of the road. Edo, there's another one. Sounds like something you take for indigestion. He looks across, sees his mate Barnaby. Barnaby. I mean, that's a real name, smugglers and highwaymen and stuff. 'Coming to the party at Jeff's tomorrow night?'

'Sure. See you there.'

'What about meeting up at the Queen's Head first?'

'Um. OK.' No point mentioning that he was thrown out last week for being very obviously underage. That's the other thing. Barnaby, Jeff, Steve, Pete, pretty well everyone, already up around six foot. And then there's five foot seven Edward, whose coming-of-age razor sits dry and underused in the tooth mug.

Some of the girls have gathered under the bus shelter, complaining about the last Chemistry lesson. Edward weighs up the alternatives of staying out and getting wet or coming back in with the gigglers. He stands his ground, sentry-like. Turns his collar up, hoping it will make him look more interesting. More water pours down his neck. He retreats under the shelter, his back to the girls, staring outwards.

'Hello Edward.' The voice, overflowing with coy tease, forces him to turn round. Catherine, small, black-haired, the topic of many a fantasy conversation in the lunch queue. She was safely off-limits, under the arm of tall, good-looking, and therefore deeply hated Johnny, Captain of the Under-17s. She's grinning at him from the centre of the group. The other girls look on, waiting for the moment to explode with laughter.

'Hmnn,' is all Edward can manage. He feels the colour creeping up his face as he stares at a point beyond her left ear.

'You coming to Jeff's then?'

'Mmnn.' Vigorous nodding. Edward hopes the passage of air over his face will cool it. It doesn't. Already, he can hear the little snorts and rumbles of the forthcoming avalanche of laughter.

Catherine gazes at him, eyes wide.

'Well, I'll see you there. Maybe we can have a dance.'

'Mmnn. Great.' At last, a real word. 'That's, um, yea…'

With a roar like a marauding lion, the bus pulls in. The moment it stops, Edward is on and heading upstairs to the front, as far away as possible. He sits alone, staring through the raindrops on the window. Giggling explodes every few minutes from behind him. He's certain it's aimed at him. At last, after a journey that seems to have taken twice the usual time, he's at his stop. He swings out of his seat and hurries to the stairs. Three of the girls are still there, though not Catherine.

'Bye, Edward,' they trill in unison.

'Bye.'

He misses his footing on the top stair and skids down, grabbing frantically at the rail. He just manages to steady himself and runs down and out to another explosion of laughter.

He stares into the bathroom mirror, a tube of Clearasil in his hand. Had to happen now, two hours before Jeff's party. The large red lump on his neck pulsates. Too risky to squeeze, just make it angrier. He smears the Clearasil on it. Makes little difference.

'Mum, where are my light blue jeans?' he yells down from the landing.

'In the wash,' echoes back.

'But I need them tonight.'

'So, I'm supposed to be a mind reader? Wear the dark blue ones.'

'That's not what I want. They're all baggy.'

His mother's head appears in the hallway. She gives him the patient sigh.

'Edward, don't be so obsessed with appearance. You are who you are. Just be yourself and you'll be fine.'

'God, Mum, you just don't get it.'

'Right. I was never young, of course.'

Edward goes into his room, stares dejectedly at his wardrobe. Eventually, he pulls out a pair of green trousers that he last wore at a family wedding six months ago and, despite them being hardly flared at all, hauls them on.

He shouts goodbye as he heads for the door.

'When will you be back?'

'Dunno. About midnight.'

The living room door opens, his dad appears.

'Dad, I'm in a real hurry.'

'No later than midnight. And here's a fiver for a cab if you miss the last bus. Give me the change tomorrow.'

'Thanks, Dad. See you.'

He aims to get to The Queen's Head just too late to have to deal with the ignominy of the barmaid refusing him but when the bus drops him there's still plenty of time. So he lingers, looking in the shop windows.

'Hey, Edo, since when were you interested in women's dresses?' Barnaby's cheerful voice behind him.

'No, I just…'

'Whatever, you coming? I'm dying for a quick pint.'

'Um, yea, right. OK.'

They go into the noise and heat and smoke of the pub, spot the others in a corner, nursing their drinks.

'Hi guys, just found Edward here drooling over the dresses in that shop on the corner. Pervy or what?'

'No, I wasn't, I mean, I was just…oh, never mind, what the hell.'

'Don't worry, old son, your secret's safe with us.'

Yeah, thought Edward, until Monday morning, then it's on public broadcast.

'So,' Barnaby rubs his hands together, 'I'll just get myself a drink. You coming, Edo?'

'Actually, if I give you the money, do you mind getting me one? Just a half. I mean, seems pointless, two of us queuing.'

Barnaby's eyebrows arch up. He sees Edward's embarrassed face and bows deeply. 'Your wish is my command.'

Edward gratefully hands over the fiver that his dad gave him and sits with the others, his back towards the bar.

Steve looks up and grins. 'Seriously good zit you've got there, old son.'

Edward's hand flies to his neck. 'Shit, is it that visible?'

'Only from Mars.'

'Don't worry,' advises Pete, 'just turn up your collar. People will think you're cool.'

Sniggers all round.

'Here you go,' Barnaby appears at his shoulder with a pint glass. 'Get that down you.'

'I said just a half.'

'Did you? Never mind, you'll manage.'

Edward takes a deep breath and swigs from his glass, just manages to stop himself choking.

Barnaby checks his watch. 'Better get going in ten minutes or so. Don't want to miss first pickings.'

'First pickings?' Edward feels, as he often feels, that there's a foreign language being spoken around him.

'Jeff's got a younger sister. Mucho crumpeta there tonight.'

Edward grabs his glass and takes another big swig.

A few more minutes psyching up about the girls, then Steve claps his hands together.

'Right, come on. Bird-hunting time. Get it down you, Ed.'

Edward looks at his glass, still more than half full. Out of the corner of his eye he sees his nemesis barmaid circulating, picking up empties. He leaps to his feet, glass in hand and turns to face her. She looks up and comes steaming over.

'I thought I told you last week to get out of here. You'll lose us our licence. Now put that down and get lost.'

Gratefully, Edward accepts the lesser of two ignominies, puts down the unwanted beer and makes for the door. The others follow, jeering.

'We'll have to get you a false moustache.'

'Next time it's ginger pop for you.'

'Have you heard about those built-up shoes?'

Edward, relieved that he's not looking at two hours of hiccoughs, belching, incoherence and constant visits to the loo, accepts everything they throw at him.

'I wanna be your lover, baby, I wanna be your man'. The depressingly unobtainable lyrics vibrate around the house. Edward has been standing in the kitchen by the drinks table, soft drinks only, thank God, for forty-five minutes, having the sort of animated conversation that you only have when you know you should be doing something much braver.

'Edward, there you are.'

The slightly slurred voice carries over the noise.

'Hi, Catherine. Aren't you with Johnny?'

She sways in front of him, waving her arms dismissively.

'Johnny's being a prick. And don't call me Catherine. Only my mum calls me that.'

'What do you want to be called, then?'

'Dunno, Kate, Katy, Cathy, hate them all really.'

'Know how you feel. How about Cilla?'

She bathes him in a lopsided grin. 'Cilla? Yea, why not. And I'll call you, let's see, Ringo.'

'OK, Cilla.'

'OK, Ringo.'

They grin at each other. Edward, realising with a sense of panic that things are going well, desperately tries to think of what to say next and fails. In the other room, The Spencer Davis Group thrash their way into 'Gimme Some Lovin''. Catherine jumps up and down.

'Ooh. Love this one. Come on, let's have that dance.'

She grabs his hand. Hers is clammy and sticky but, at this moment, Edward wouldn't trade it for a handful of diamonds.

As Catherine leaps and gyrates in front of him, Edward looks around to see who's watching and hops gently from foot to foot with little waves of his arms.

'Come on, Ringo,' she shouts up at him. 'Get into the music!'

And suddenly, like with the rain on his face, it connects. Everyone else disappears and there's just him, her and the music, in him, through him, a part of him. Every atom of his being moves with the sound. The Who, Four Tops, Small Faces and Aretha Franklin control them both, the electricity passes between the two of them at a primal level. He sees her hair swirl across her face, glimpses of eyes, teeth, shoulders, arms waving, legs prancing. They are one.

Then, suddenly, the music slows. Engelbert Humperdinck wails plaintively at him and he's back in the present, aware that everyone is looking at them. He sees Johnny at the back, glaring. The most natural thing in the world would be to take Catherine in his arms for a smooch. Natural, but too high a mountain to climb. He stands, waving his arms around slowly, as if this is the thing he would most like to do in the world right now. Catherine solves the problem, lurching forward into him and grabbing on. Her head goes onto his shoulder. It fits nicely. Tentatively, he puts his arms around her.

She looks up at him.

'That was great,' he ventures.

She reaches up and whispers in his ear. 'Don't feel very well. Can we get some air?'

Hoping this is code, he guides her as quickly as he can to the French windows and out onto the little terrace. Notices a couple of the lads give him the thumbs up.

As soon as they are outside, Catherine doubles up and is sick, noisily and copiously. Edward recoils, then leans in and gently pulls her hair back away from her face, making sure his legs are well out of the firing line. He stands, slave-like, waiting.

Eventually, Catherine is finished.

'Sorry,' she gasps. 'Wine, I think. Shouldn't have.'

Jeff's mum appears out of the darkness.

'Come along, dear,' she says briskly. 'Let's get you cleaned up.'

And they're gone. He is left with the smell and the knowledge that, somehow, everything has changed.

He wanders back in.

'Alright, Ed?'

'You were moving there, man.'

'Nice one.'

He smiles and goes through to the hall. Gathering up his coat, he opens the front door. Looks up. It's just beginning to rain again. He realises that he didn't get any change from Barnaby. He sets off to walk home, face up to the rain.

THE ARTIST'S LIFE

The morning sun pushes through the cracked shutters like a burglar. Coming downstairs into the small front room, Annabel winces. Two bottles of the rough local wine last night have left her with a pounding head. The local farmers and vineyard owners love to tell her that sunlight is the gift from God; this morning, she finds that hard to believe.

She looks around. The shafts of light fall mockingly on the pile of canvases stacked neatly against the wall, all his, none hers. The room smells of sweat and turpentine. She stumbles through to the kitchen, still cool away from the sun. Pushing aside the pile of dirty dishes in the sink, she fills the kettle. The pipe thumps and clatters.

'Oh, shut up, for God's sake,' she mutters, 'you'll wake him.' The water spurts out erratically, bouncing off the blackened kettle and splashing the art college logo on the front of her t-shirt. She feels the tears start to well. Her hand shakes as she strikes a match for the gas, which flares up before subsiding into a blue-yellow hiss.

She shivers. Reaching for the shawl that hangs on the back of the door, she wraps herself in it and walks out to the small back yard, stands motionless, staring at the pot of withered herbs. She had planted them, just a few weeks earlier, full of plans for the meals that she would cook for her lover; at that time the word still made her squirm with pleasure. With a puzzled frown she recalls that dream of shopping in the market, walking back with the fresh baguettes and salads, feeding her man, the artist, as they talked of art and sat long into the evening under the wide Provençal sky. This had been the promise when he'd invited, no, ordered her to come out for the summer. But promises have a way of losing their colour, fading to shades of grey.

She hears a door slam upstairs and runs back into the kitchen. To her horror, she realises that she has not put the kettle onto the stove. Grabbing the lid, she slams it down onto the kettle. It bounces off onto the floor. She hears footsteps on the stairs. Scrabbling under the stove amid the curling scraps of vegetables, her fingers find it. She turns to jump up and cracks her head on the edge of the table. The shock and pain force her back down, curled on the floor, her hands cradling her head as the tears flow.

'Oh, for fuck's sake. *Now* what have you done?' The Sheffield accent of which he is so proud grates across the room.

Her blurred eyes take in two naked legs in the doorway. Against her will, she remembers her disappointment when she saw him naked for the first time. His body looked rounded and inviting when swathed in jeans and a leather jacket, lounging in the darkness of a North London pub after his first lecture. But in the harsh electric light of his cramped office at the art college, it was pale and starting to sag. When she insisted on making love in the dark, he had mocked her middle-class shyness and she had let him.

But those had been good times. She felt singled out, special. She knew she could paint; distinction at A Level and praise from her tutors confirmed her skill, and now this man, this real artist was taking a special interest. If she occasionally felt uncomfortable about his constant criticism of her work, she could tell herself that she needed to be pushed to get better. When the criticism became personal, well, he was just having a bad day. And anyway, he always apologised afterwards, in his way. When it moved on to him stopping her socialising with her contemporaries, well, that was just about focusing on her art. She doesn't remember actually deciding to come to Provence for the summer, but here she was, and the only brushes she had picked up in the last three weeks were his, which she had to clean each evening.

Now, in the dimness of the kitchen, she looks up at the legs, their veins blue and knotted. Forcing her eyes quickly past what he insists on calling his pleasure zone, she counts the folds of his stomach, the thin scattering of curls between his sagging breasts and up to his lank hair, not yet pulled back into a ponytail but hanging grey and greasy over the unshaven face. The pale blue eyes that had so transfixed her and most of the other first year students are now watery and bloodshot.

'Where's my coffee?'

'I wish you'd put some clothes on. There's people walking past.'

'Stuff 'em. Bring some thrill into their boring little lives. Where's my fucking coffee?'

'I'm sorry, Don, I just…'

'Sorry? Sorry? How many times do I have to tell you? You are here for two reasons, Annabel.' He always made her name sound like an insult. 'One, so that I can get my artistic rocks off whenever I can't be bothered to go out for something better and two, to keep me supplied with coffee and alcohol. You're pretty crap at the first and now it seems you can't even manage the second.'

'Fine, I'll go home then.'

He steps forward and with a speed that shocks her, slaps her hard across the face.

'You'll go home when I tell you to go home. Not that Mummy and Daddy in their manicured one sweet sherry before Sunday lunch house in Guildford will want you back. Not after you've been tainted by big bad northern artist. And Jeremy from the Conservative Club won't want you now, will he, Annabel? Now, make me a coffee and then stay out of my fucking way.'

He grabs a pack of cigarettes off the table and turns back to the front room, slamming the door behind him. She hears him walk over to the neatly stacked canvases, rummage through them and discard four or five in a pile on the floor.

She rubs her head while waiting for the kettle to boil. She hears another crash then silence from the other room. Each beat of her heart thumps pain though her head. Reaching up, she takes a bottle of paracetamol from the cupboard. Unscrewing the top, she shakes two, then four, then ten tablets into her hand. For a long time, she stands looking at the pile of small white pills. It would be so easy. She raises her hand, bends forward. There is a sharp whistle as the kettle boils. She jerks back, dropping several tablets onto the floor, and turns off the gas. Grabbing a glass from the draining board, she rinses out the wine dregs, pours some cold water from the tap into it and swallows down just two tablets. The glass is painful against her lip, which is starting to swell. Then she makes the coffee. Just before taking a mug into him she pauses, leans forward and carefully spits into the cup.

She steps through the doorway to the front room, bracing herself. By now, he is usually hunched on his stool, intimately locked into his canvas, excluding her completely, though this does not stop the ranting. But this time, he is lying on his back in the middle of the room. She hears, instead of the expected insults, a strange rattling gasp. His mouth is moving, the lips a shade of blue, but no words are forming. A hand, the one that slapped her a minute ago, reaches waveringly towards her. His eyes look up at her. She sees terror in them, as they beg her for help. The coffee drops to the floor as she runs across the room to him. She kneels.

'Oh, God. Don't worry, Don. I'll go and get the doctor. I'll be as quick as I can.'

She runs back into the kitchen and grabs up the shawl from the floor, where it had fallen when she banged her head. As she turns to go, she sees the paracetamol bottle on its side, the tablets fanning out from its neck.

She has to step over him to get to the door. As she does so, his fingers scrabble at her jeans, trying to hold her back. She pulls away and leaves without another word.

Outside, the sun hits hard. But this time she does not flinch. Turning right, she walks purposefully up the narrow path. On one side, the ground drops away, offering a view across the valley to the mountains beyond. The houses stand along the other side, dug into the hillside and leaning back from the drop.

She walks steadily up the hill. The doctor's house is the last one before the square at the top. Without breaking her step, she walks straight past the big red front door and on into the square.

She takes a seat in front of the café, where she can see back down the hill. The pain in her head is starting to ease. The houses are scattered along the curving path, reminding her of a broken string of dusty pearls that she had once found thrown into the back of a drawer in her mother's dressing table. At this time of the morning, for a few short minutes, the sun hits the houses full on. Soon it will move on and they will slump back, ordinary in their flaked paint, their cracked walls and their satellite dishes, but for this moment they stand up like stars in the spotlight, ready for the applause, ready for the artist.

She thinks she may stay for a while, now that...... now that things have changed. The waiter approaches. She is aware that he is staring at her red face and swelling lip.

'Bonjour, Mademoiselle. Ça va?'

'Oui, merci, Jacques. Ça va très bien.'

This piece was inspired by a short story by Heinrich Böll, which I read as a teenager and which has stayed with me.

MY UNCOUNTED LOVE

They patched me up as best they could. Then they flew me back home, away from the flies and the sand and the bombs. Did a bit more patching up, but I got the feeling it was all getting a bit half-hearted.

After that, they couldn't get rid of me fast enough. They were polite about it, in their way. Like the time I woke up and found some leaflets by my bed with, 'Life after the Army' in big, bold type. Subtle or what? It was like 'Thanks for the last twelve years of your life. Sorry about the broken bits but here's your pension. Not enough to live on but, hey, nice to have a pension at twenty-nine, isn't it?'

Anyway, it was clear that I wasn't any use to them any more so, as soon as I could walk, if you can call it walking, they sent me off to a company that recruits ex-service people, what they insisted on calling vets. Seems they're a branch of some American outfit. Bloody Americans, what do they know about fighting? I could tell you some stories, but this is not the place.

Said they have special jobs at this company for semi-ambulatories. That's what I am now, apparently, a semi-ambulatory. Not a man, not a guy who used to play football up at Headstone Manor, not Charlie who goes to the pub on Friday night. Just a semi-bloody-ambulatory. So, they put me in a box beside the steps, you know, the ones that come down from Harrow station towards the shopping centre. Thirty-seven steps altogether. I know, because I have to come down them every morning from the tube. Twenty-two up from the platform, thirty-seven down to the road. Bet the guy who designed them didn't get a pain with every step, like a stiletto knifing up his spine and into his brain. Bet the guy who sent me here doesn't live in fear of falling every time he changes levels. Didn't think of that, did they? Help for heroes? I don't think so.

Anyway, there I am in my little box. It's quite a warm box; it's got a light and a little heater, so not bad. My job is to count the people. That's it, no more. Just to count the people. Count them as they go up and count them as they go down.

So, I settled into it, ticking my little boxes as neat as can be. My army training taught me to do things properly, so I really worked at it. To start with. Pages of little boxes, red ticks for the adults, blue for the kids; every passer-by recorded, changed from human being to a mark with a biro. Not that any of them know, of course; too busy with their own lives to notice me. Some of the kids stop and stare at me, but they are hustled away by their parents.

There was one person I never counted, even when I was doing it properly. My uncounted love, I call her. I watch her, every morning, as she comes down the stairs. She has a sort of bouncy way of jumping from step to step that makes her ponytail swing from side to side as she goes. She likes to wear pink, I've noticed, bright tracksuit tops and, now that it's getting cold, a pink scarf. I haven't seen a lot of bright colours in my world and, I can tell you, it's like watching a rainbow walking. She works in Greggs, you know, the sandwich place, just down the end of the road. I see her coming back in the evening with bags with their name on. Leftovers, I suppose.

In fact, that's what she reminds me of, that statue down there opposite Greggs, the one of the girl skipping. Same sort of bounce, like she'd prefer to be skipping but doesn't quite have the nerve. She always seems so clean, so happy. There's no way she's going to be a statistic, not on my watch.

And don't they just love their statistics. Some little spotty geek comes in at the end of each day to pick up the sheets from me and he's positively drooling. I asked him once what they did with the numbers. Not that I was interested. I just felt I had to make some kind of conversation with him. He's the sort of guy who probably speaks fluent Klingon, but obviously wasn't very good at communicating with anything human. Anyway, he gives me this great spiel about analysis and government statistics, something to do with having to justify the cost of refurbishing the entrance. I'm not really sure; I'd stopped listening by then. I remember wondering what would happen if they didn't justify the costs. Would the government make them take the steps away and put them up somewhere else? Or maybe just put in thirty and everyone would have to jump down the last bit. Or would the local council just have to write out fifty times, 'I must not build steps that cannot be justified'?

So, I thought I might as well help them along a bit. After the first couple of weeks, I knew roughly how many were coming through each day anyway, so I just put down the average numbers, plus or minus a bit so it wasn't too obvious and then I started to boost them a bit. Bring a little more sunshine into their dull lives. They were so happy, bless them. After that, I never bothered to count anyone anymore and I had time to do the crossword and the Sudoku.

They checked up on me last week. Sent a man in to sit beside me and count too. All day we sat there with our pads, making our little marks. I had to really concentrate but at the end of it, I had only one less than him. Like I said, there's no way she's going to be a statistic.

They were very pleased with me. Sent me a little letter thanking me for my 'exemplary work'. And they've given me a promotion. Starting Monday, I'm going to get some poor bloody school leaver to help. Why they need two people to do one job is something I'm not clear about but why should I care? They want us to count bicycles as well but that's not too difficult. They're not allowed on the tube anyway at rush hour, so I'll have plenty of time to take a break. Maybe I'll pop down to Gregg's for a coffee occasionally. Yes, I'd like that.

DOG AND THE MAN

A spring day, promising warmth but not yet delivering, a teaser of a day that has lured just one or two people out onto the beach. They've soon turned back to the café, flapping their arms around them as they stagger, penguin-like, over the pebbles.

Hasn't stopped him, though. He is out on that beach rain or shine, him and Dog. If anyone is pushy enough to ask, he'll agree, with a shrug, that it's not a very original name for a canine friend, but he can't be doing with this ridiculous indulgence of naming animals as if they were people. And there's something else. With his rich knowledge of English literature, he has at his fingertips all of the most evocative names in the world. But literature has turned its back on him, so why should he give it air. He never explains any of this to intrusive questioners, of course, just puts on his schoolmasterly voice and announces, 'He's a dog. Drinks from the toilet. Licks his own balls. End of story. Dog.'

They usually go away after that.

Not that he talks to many people.

He makes his steady way along the edge of the sea, letting the waves creep up to his feet and then withdraw like obsequious waiters. Dog, black, sleek, intense, follows his nose, hoovering his way up and down. No sound but the waves and the wind, just how he likes it.

A voice from behind carves its way through the wind.

'Hey! Mate!'

A child's voice, a boy. The man's shoulders hunch slightly. He does not turn.

'Mate! Hold on!' The voice is nearer.

A hand tugs at his coat. He freezes. Doesn't want this.

Ahead of him, Dog has stopped, head to one side, and starts to move back towards him, tail tucked down.

The man turns slowly. The boy is short, skinny, maybe ten years old, shivering in a t-shirt and jeans. His hair is spiky, full of some gunk. Behind him, standing a few feet back, is a girl, even younger. He notices the thin blue summer dress that's already too small for her, dirty blonde hair straggling across her face and onto her shoulders. The man puts on his most unwelcoming face.

'What?'

'We're lost.' There's an attempt at bravado in the slightly hoarse voice but it is overcome by a tremor. The man can see the girl's face start to crumple. Dog circles round and sits on his haunches, watching and waiting, tongue lolling. 'We came round that headland, then the tide came in and we don't know how to get back.'

'Go to the café. They'll let you phone your parents.'

'We tried. They wouldn't let us.'

'That's because you tried to nick a Mars Bar.' The girl's voice is harsh.

'Shut up.' The boy turns back to the man, eyes wide. 'I didn't.'

He's seen it all before, the professional innocence. For a moment, he's back in his study, dealing with a recalcitrant Year Sixer.

He knows the rules; no contact. That's why he's here, far from what he used to call home. He turns away.

'Can't help you. Sorry.'

He clicks his fingers. Dog jumps up and they walk off together.

'I told you he wouldn't do nothing,' he hears the girl's voice. 'None of them ever do.'

'Whatever.'

'What are we going to do? Where are we going to go?' The girl's voice rises with every question. 'I'm cold.'

'Don't worry, I'll think of something. Don't worry.'

It's the care and concern he hears in the boy's voice that makes the man stop. He closes his eyes, thinks of all the reasons why he should keep walking, then turns.

'Where are you staying?' he calls.

'The caravan park, Sunshine Court.'

'I'll call your parents.'

'They got no phone. It's bust.'

A moment's hesitation, trying not to think of the consequences.

'Come on, I'll drive you back.'

'Oh, thanks, mate.'

'But only if you stop calling me mate.'

'What do you want us to call you?'

It's a good question. Not his name, that's for sure. He shrugs.

'Just not mate, OK.'

The two children fall in step behind him.

'What's your dog's name?'

'Dog.'

'Cool.'

The man suppresses a smile.

'Does he bite?'

'Yes.'

He strides up the beach towards his house, which stands alone up near the ridge. He's aware that the children are struggling to keep up as they cross the big pebbles. He does not slow down, even though his own legs are tired and aching.

They get to the cottage, a low white building, unkempt and battered, crouching down by the road.

'Wait here, I'll get my car keys.'

He unlocks the door, reaches in for the keys, which hang on a hook just inside. Pulls the door shut.

'Can I use your toilet, please?' The girl is hopping from one leg to another.

The man sighs and opens the door again.

'Straight through, round behind the stairs. Be quick.'

He pulls the door to behind her. He is not going to be alone in the house with her.

The boy stands awkwardly, staring at his shoes. An old feeling, a need to bridge the gap, comes over the man.

'So, what year are you in? Six?'

The boy nods.

'Do you like school?'

A shrug.

'Why not?'

The boy still does not look up.

'Boring.'

That word. How many times over how many years has he heard it? He can see this boy's life planned out, ordinary and unremembered.

Dog, who has been waiting patiently to get in, to food and basket, plods past the man and pushes at the front door. It swings open and, in that instant, the man sees the young girl pick up something from the hall shelf and slip it up under her dress, tucking it into her knickers.

Before he can stop himself, he shouts.

'What do you think you're doing? Put that back.'

The girl jumps back, staring at him, silent.

He advances on her.

Dog, who had been heading through to the kitchen, comes back into the hall, watches silently.

'Put that back!' Slowly, loud and straight at her.

He is leaning down towards the girl. He knows how to make children afraid, just as he knows how to comfort them or encourage them.

The boy comes running in.

'Oy, you leave off my sister.'

'Your sister, if that's what she is, is a thief.'

'No, she's not.'

'She has taken an ornament, a brass Buddha, from that shelf and tucked it under her dress.'

'No, she ain't. You're making it up. You just wanna look at her knickers. You're a paedo, you are.'

It takes the man's breath away. Again. The pain comes roaring back. His job, his family, his reputation taken by the brazen claims of a stupid, ignorant young child, criminal at ten years old, whatever the school uniform and angelic look might have said.

The boy runs at him, kicks him on the back of the leg. The man grabs him by the t-shirt, slams him against the wall. The girl screams. Dog growls, barks, just twice, moves forward a pace.

Then silence.

The boy is lying on the floor, winded, his t-shirt torn. The girl is crouched, fumbling to get the Buddha out.

She throws it on the floor.

Dog growls softly, looking to his master for guidance.

Time stops. And the man realises that this time it's different. This time, he has nothing left to lose. This is the moment when he gets payback for all the pain, the loss, the terrible loss. Two children, no one knows where they are. Could have been swept out to sea, fallen off the cliff path. No one would know.

He sees Dog looking at him, head slightly to one side, eyebrows furrowed together.

And suddenly, he starts to laugh. He laughs because he is free. Because this whole stupid, absurd episode, its very banality, has changed tragedy to farce. Because he can feel the last ten years dropping away, a weight released.

The children look at him, scared but hopeful.

'Get out!' he shouts between guffaws.

They scrabble out through the open door. On the road, the boy turns and raises two fingers.

'Fucking paedo.'

And runs.

The man gently closes the door. Dog comes towards him, head down, tail wagging. The man reaches down and tickles his chin.

'Come on, Dog, let's get you fed. And then, maybe, think of a better name for you.'

Also by Phil Lawder

The Banker's Ex-Wife

In this comedy mystery for today, a surprise is coming to complacent, unambitious, happily divorced and not very likeable Kate Bradshaw. In fact, a lot of surprises, not many of them pleasant.

It's amazing what you learn when everything is taken away. Pouting Anastasia, possibly sister to the very solid Boris, and the mysterious Muddle open new worlds for her, as Kate discovers who she can really be.

And so, on a journey that takes her through Job Centres, gangsters, casinos, a brothel, street fighting, attempted kidnap and a nice picnic in the Derbyshire hills, Kate gets to understand the world, and herself, a little better.

She may even end up liking herself; you may even end up liking her.

The Old Buggers' Brigade

A contemporary thriller, a dystopia that feels all too possible.

The streets of Britain are no longer safe. Stirred up by ambitious politicians, the younger generation have started to attack the rich oldies.

Jenny is retired, wealthy and bored in a polite suburb of London. She seizes the chance to fight back as part of the Old Buggers' Brigade, and to feel the excitement that she is longing for.

But things are never what they seem, and she is quickly drawn into a world of danger and deception that threatens the lives of her family.

Edges

A collection of poems about the magic of the ordinary, the unspoken undertow of relationships and the quiet desperation of the suburbs, that strange human geometry where edges clash, merge and intersect.

This is a world you will recognise, a world of supermarkets, the weather and random chance. And love – confused, hopeful, frustrated, uncertain love.

ACKNOWLEDGMENTS

My thanks go

- to Siobhan Curham for her editing skills and support
- to Susannah Straughan for her highly professional and knowledgeable proof reading
- to Colin Robinson for his patient and highly creative work on the cover
- to Richard Cutler for his wise advice
- and to all my fellow writers who listened with patience and gave me their views with generosity and constructive support.

Printed in Great Britain
by Amazon

31415544R00070